Galactic Battlefront Chronicles
of a UO Soldier

Galactic Battlefront Chronicles of a UO Soldier

By: Don Jastrebski

ISBN 978-0-615-76754-3

Introduction

Some of you may have visited our website www.gbuniverse.com and some of you may not. For those who have not feel free to head over there and check out the prequel story, "Siege of the Golden City" for free if you'd like to catch up. If not, go ahead and jump right in with this first book, *Chronicles of a UO Soldier.* You can also explore and read detailed descriptions of characters, weapons, planets, races, and many other facets of the GB universe on our website. Whatever you decide to do, make sure you take a look at the most exciting new sci-fi saga around, Galactic Battlefront. Also, we'll be adding a new short-story every few months and bringing you news on TV and Movie possibilities.

In the years that have passed since the Mordots attempted their siege of the Golden City, the Universe has been plagued with an onslaught of death and devastation. Universal crime rates had already been on a steady rise for nearly a century and yet they still have somehow managed to double within the last 5 years. Senseless acts of violence were the most mind-boggling of all. A Colton Princess had been held captive for nearly a year and although payment for her safe return had been offered several times she was eventually assassinated, her body being put on public display by her captors. Terrorist attacks and insurgent takeovers have become all the more rampant, and sometimes it seems as though the Universal Order(UO) is dealing with an out-of-control situation on a daily basis. Pirated vessels and gangs were popping up in virtually every inhabited solar system at an accelerated rate; intergalactic freighters now have more than a one in five chance of being seized. The UO's necessity to deal with the larger problems now persistent in the Verse has allowed the younger, more ambitious generation of criminals to test and capitalize on the parameters of UO authority.

With such dysfunction and so many new grievances popping up throughout the Verse, the UO is spread exceedingly thin.

Sometimes only a pair or in a few cases a lone soldier is dispatched to tend to the mediation of an entire problematic galaxy(often dozens if not hundreds of claims, disagreements, skirmishes, and grievances). Mace Crimson and Brutus Callous are two of the most overworked soldiers in the Order and although many units have been putting in extra time, these two are unmatched. They've shown their skills as mediators as well as combatants time and time again while also displaying supreme judgment and assessment in various problematic situations. They've gained some esteem within the UO, but Mace has also taken significant flack over a theory he has openly shared with many of his fellow soldiers. Mace is under the belief that a mastermind universal crimelord is in control of all the recent plights of the Verse; he believes that this mastermind has been coordinating and manipulating the actions and will of many civilians, governments, criminal enterprises, and even the UO itself. His instincts tell him that this crimelord may in actuality be a legendary warlord who has long been thought dead, an individual simply named Narel. It is a proposal that has been met with extreme hostility by his superiors and Mace has no real evidence to support it; mostly just hearsay, inaccuracies, and strange coincidences. Either way the veteran soldier's gut tell him that there is something really wrong with the Verse and he is determined to uncover the threat and dissolve it any way he can.

Table of Contents

The Bridge of Valeena

The year is 2517, Mace and Brutus are part of a large-scale UO mission. They have been frantically searching a solar system called Galfin Bena after gathering several verified leads that Narel's army is using the system as a liaison to his base planets. Galfin Bena contains large populations of various races and refugees making it fairly easy to disguise illicit operations. Mace and around two hundred other UO operatives are currently present within Galfin Bena, all focused on the same goal; to further uncover the connection between the Org and Narel, while constantly searching for clues that will help narrow down the thrifty warlord's actual whereabouts. At this time most of the Verse is still in denial of his very existence; many leaderships including the UO commander's council actively contest that modern stories of the seemingly immortal tyrant are nothing more than a folklore trend. After all, it has always been public knowledge that Narel was killed long ago by the great UO Commander, Tagithus Hashin. Stories of Narel's previous resurrections have been rumored for centuries, although in those instances there had been no proof that he'd actually been killed. On the most recent occasion however, there was no doubting the fact that Tagithus had destroyed him, and the remains of Narel were incinerated within a closed plasma chamber. Such certain obliteration would also ensure that no traces of the warlord would remain, if he were to return this time it would be something of note.

That was crazy talk anyway, thought to be brought into the Verse by the lower class of society, blaming the cause of their troubles on some immortal villain. Every credible member of universal culture with a sense of class knew that no being nor race no matter how powerful had ever been able to resurrect the deceased. No, even to beings of sub par intelligence, basic logic and common sense told them that Narel was long gone, never to return again.

Only Mace and a handful of others were outraged at how so many could blindly dismiss such a possible threat without even giving it a proper investigation, and even they did not fully understand the level of fear and panic brought on by this one sadistic individual. The entire Universe seems to dread his memory with intolerable fear, leaving those far removed from his areas of activity blind to said activities. Hierarchy can only succeed if the information flowing upward is well received; it should never matter who brings the matter at hand to light, all that should matter is finding out the truth.

As opposed to the average civilian and high ranking UO officials; some UO field soldiers over the past few years have come to the conclusion that Narel does currently exist, and is at this time roaming the Verse with goals unknown. It has become a common yet unspoken theory that those who report up the chain of command with ideas or leads on the subject are met with harsh scrutiny and unfair criticism. It's a topic where those who pursue the truth must speak to only those who will listen. This is a significant problem because most of the UO personnel who can encounter Narel and his followers are ranked no higher than Sergeant; with the majority being Privates who most frequently patrol the Verse.

Nonetheless, there has been some progress in recent years. Since the capture and final escape of Zade Malin, several of Mace's superiors including Lieutenant Gil Lang and Major Valin Parra have come to openly support the idea that The Org and Narel are actually one colossal threat. This has been able to help Mace and others begin preliminary investigations. Still, none of the UO Commanders have been convinced of the plot, a major obstacle that needs to be overcome if real progress is ever to be made. Without the Commander's Council putting their weight behind the investigation on this alliance, it will inevitably run out of steam. The trail has already gone cold since Zade's escape and Mace has been hunting down even the smallest leads with no result. Trying to catch Narel proved to be like trying to capture smoke in a wind tunnel; Galfin Bena is one of the few places his pawns have even been tracked and may be the only place to spark a lead.

Of the numerous agents working for Narel who have been followed or pursued into this system, not one has led to anyone or anything of importance. Uncovering the identities of some high ranking officials working for Narel is a crucial step in assessing the overall threat, yet the UO's never even spoken to one.

What is known about Narel's army is this; it consists almost entirely of a specially trained group of warriors who are easily recognizable to most inhabitants of the Verse due to the countless stories and folklore that precede them. They can usually be identified by the numerous scars and disfigurements covering their bodies, remnants of past battles as well as Narel's brutal training tactics; scars that are so gruesome and abundant that they can often times be seen even when the soldier is fully armored. These ruthless warriors are known around the universe by the name Nexcins, which was given to them several centuries ago by a race that Narel enslaved and then eradicated. Nexcin armor is usually covered with razor sharp spikes and protrusions, always all black in color even when long faded, and more often than not is worn down and overly abused. They're widely considered to be the most loyal and brutal warriors in the Verse. Nexcins can be of any race or descent, although this sometimes becomes hard to determine as no matter what color their skin appears at the start of their training it will turn to a faded black long before they achieve rank. This is another side effect of the warlord's vicious initiation tactics and it is said that the skin is charred to sever any remaining connection the being had to their previous race. From then on they are known to the Verse and themselves solely as a Nexcin. They view Narel as a god and are more than willing to sacrifice themselves for him at any time. As mentioned before, the UO has tracked some of these Nexcins to Galfin Bena. However, once they reach it a vast majority of them manage to evade detection and capture, seeming to disappear once inside the busy system. The few Nexcin Soldiers the UO has been able to close in on subtly and quickly inject an acidic compound into their veins, instantly committing suicide at the first sign of impending capture. This acidic compound is set within an automated syringe which is placed inside the armor of the Nexcin; it administers a hypodermic injection instantly when pressed firmly against the skin. So basically at the press of a button, the Nexcin can choose to die painlessly rather than risk divulging any information to the enemy. It should be noted that a Nexcin will only use this in a seemingly hopeless situation and not all will even use it then; they are fearsome and fearless warriors who will fight insurmountable odds for their cause. Mace himself has not run into any Nexcins on Galfin Bena and despite numerous leads he has yet to come face to face with one at all.

Mace currently sits inside Lieutenant Lang's mobile office aboard the mid-sized starship Centon-7, waiting to speak with his superior about the progress of their current mission. He stares out the window at the cosmic blanket of stars, they are so numerous yet so distant and it looked as though space were painted with a faint white glow. He is surprised to see Major Parra enter the room alongside the Lieutenant.

Mace stands at attention until Major Parra speaks, "At ease soldier, I heard why you've called this meeting today and decided to tag along. I respect your opinion because of the job you've done in the past; it's not every day that I'd listen to a Sergeant. We need to open the commanders' eyes if we wanna find out what's really going on. This operation on Galfin Bena was my first attempt at that, but the way it's going I don't know if I'll be approved for another one. You're the one who blew the whistle on Narel to begin with, so tell me how to find him."

Mace responds, "Well sir, the truth of the matter is we don't have much left to work with out here. The Nexcins use Galfin Bena as a hub for their army, but they rarely occupy it for extended periods of time. They remain covert for the duration of their stay, traveling in small groups and blending in with the lower class, refugee-filled population which makes them hard to track. The good news is, this mission has made us certain that the Nexcin Army uses these planets frequently, so the system must be situated within a critical or at least significant part of their overall structure. There must be a base or supply planet nearby and most likely more than one. The truth is, we need to search surrounding systems in order to find a larger, but likely more secluded meeting ground. One that the Nexcins would consider safe and where we can pin them down without any civilian population. This will give us a much better chance at capturing live Nexcin prisoners."

The Major replies, "It's a shame we need them that way…I'd prefer to stack up dead Nexcins before losing one more soldier in an attempt to bring them in. I'm impressed with your analysis though Sergeant, you seem to have a better grasp on the situation than any other soldier I've come across…and that includes commanders."

Lieutenant Lang looks to the Major, "I told you he was something".

"Still", replies the Major, "my superiors won't just let me pick up and leave, they need results and that means Nexcin prisoners to answer questions about Narel. He's been terrorizing the Verse for centuries and we don't even know what race he is."

Mace interrupts, "I don't see why race even matters in his case. From accounts I've managed to piece together he's described as a large, pitch-black-skinned, bipedal being with deep red eyes. He's around eight feet tall and the width of his shoulders are almost equivalent to his height. Some tales say he has two thumbs on each hand, which is why he is so skilled with a plasma staff; not to mention the endless list of telekinetic powers legend claims he possesses. He seems to be a being unto himself, characterized as a race of his own, unlike and unmatched by any other individual in the Verse. Perhaps he is the last surviving member or maybe he is the only one of his kind. There are innumerable possible explanations for him all seeming farfetched or downright preposterous until you read his file, then they all seem just as plausible as the next. His race doesn't mean a thing seeing as how we have detailed descriptions of him. No matter where he's from, this warlord's become far too big of a threat to ignore anymore Major."

The Major seems further impressed, "We're in agreement soldier, but like I said we can't spare many men. I've already assured the Council that Galfin Bena was the perfect location for this operation, so unless we wanna pull the plug on the whole mission I need to keep almost everyone here. You and your partner can begin a search of the outlying systems; any planets you think may have Nexcin activity. I'll send out additional pairs once they free up, I'm still hoping to catch a lucky break here though."

Mace confidently replies, "I'll start with the Delinon System, they have three banking planets and profitable ore mines on every moon. It would be more than a desirable target for Narel so it's as good a place as any to start."

Major Parra says, "You can leave as soon as you've loaded your supplies sergeant. Oh and one more thing, we've recently been experiencing an increase in terrorist activities taking place in UO friendly areas across the Verse."

Mace intervenes, "I don't think that would be Narel, with as long as he's been preparing for this I doubt he'd risk exposure with low-impact tactics such as terrorism."

"Our analysts came to the same conclusion", responds Major Parra, "but they believe that the Org would. The Organization has become so widespread and well hidden that they can attack UO and ally installations within systems that they control practically free of risk. Often times their probably even collecting insurance settlements off of attacks on structures they at least partially own, but subsequently destroy. The truth is, the Org has become so well connected and deeply-rooted across the Verse anymore, terrorism would be the perfect tactic."

Mace replies, "Maybe, but what would they have to gain?"

Major Parra continues, "That's what I'm trying to get to, you see we think that the Org is orchestrating these attacks on behalf of Narel. It's my personal belief that the two sides are in fact working together and are actively pursuing a plan to seize control of the entire Verse. These small, strategic attacks figure to be a test; they are in a sense checking the parameters of UO intervention which is why we must remain as unpredictable as possible. I just thought I would let you in on that little theory, it's a lot easier to keep our eyes open when we have an idea of what to look for. Now go and look after yourself Sergeant, we need you on the road."

"Yes, sir" says Mace as he heads to tell Brutus of their new mission and prepare for departure.

Brutus isn't nearly as excited about the new mission as Mace is, but he is as intrigued as anyone about the possible connection between Narel and the Org. He knows there's no better person to uncover this connection than Mace and he would always have his lifelong friend's back. So not very long after Mace received his orders from Major Parra the two set out on their way.

They take a UO fighter out of Centon 7's main hangar and head for the Delinon System, once they arrive they'll begin their search for Nexcins and the Org. There is a fair amount of inhabited space in between their current location and Delinon so they'll have to travel a little slower than usual. It is dangerous to move through even unpopulated solar systems at high velocity, unlike in open space where craft can travel at near light speeds without worrying about the possibility of collision, matter-filled star systems are quite the obstacle. This is due to the mechanical make-up of all long-range craft, particularly a device called the mercury gaphoid. This mechanism consists of numerous circular electromagnets which spin around a dense core of mercury. The resulting processes effectively warp spacetime and allow for steady, long distance space travel. This spacetime distortion is a necessity, but also can be disastrous for a ship as well as bystanders if initiated too close to a planet or hub. Ships do not actually travel faster than the speed of light, yet along with the mercury gaphoid, high yield propulsion systems such as anti-matter thrusters make it seem like they do, cutting corners in a sense. Interstellar voyages would have never become so widespread if not for this little gadget, other alternatives such as wormhole generators are available, but are far too expensive to ever be mass-produced by any race.

The two soldiers play several card games and even practice plasma staff duels to pass the time while they travel. The two sleep in shifts so that there is always someone watching the controls and orientation of the ship. The long hours of space travel are one of the main drawbacks to a UO soldier's life. When your jurisdiction is the Universe, no distress call is ever right down the street and none is too far away.

They coast through a couple star systems that are uneventful and are not hassled by any local governments or patrols. After more than half a day of travel their ship comes to the last system lying in their way.

Mace jumps into the cockpit and grabs the controls; he's getting anxious and wants to maneuver around this last detour promptly. "Let's get through here, then we can use a little anti-matter and get to Delinon in no time."

He switches to manual controls and looks ahead where he takes notice of something odd, a huge cloud of gas, resembling that of an early nebula during star formation sits ominously out in open space. The gargantuan cloud is set into an orb shape with numerous stringy protrusions branching out from each side; looking similar to the way solar flares breech a star's surface, arcing back into itself to create an arch. The sight is spectacular, unlike any gas formation they had ever seen and it seemingly had no reason to be there. The cloud glows in many places, exhibiting an array of colors with the majority showing a yellowish-green tint.

Brutus says, "You ever see something like that?"

"Can't say that I have", responds Mace, "But it can't be natural, there aren't the elements nor the conditions for something like that out here".

They don't have long to admire the anomalous sight as out of the corner of his eye Mace notices a large grouping of ships sitting in a poorly organized encampment formation. Mace can't believe his eyes as he looks upon a primitive planet called Kutchatar. The information on this large orange planet pops up on Mace's view screen and indicates that its inhabitants are a low-level race with little technology; yet he can clearly identify a large starship orbiting the planet along with what looks like a convoy of cruisers and warships. Mace immediately recognizes the design of the starship from his days of fighting in the Centaur-Sirian War, when he first joined the UO. They belonged to his enemy during the conflict, the Sirians. These cities that the Sirians call starships are massive, unlike any other model in the Verse and hard to mistake. They look like two massive octagons, each the size of a normal starship itself with a long, thick chamber connecting them. That chamber was the easiest way to identify the vessel as it gives off a red glow which results from a massive amount of condensed plasma which it conceals underneath. All Sirian plasma gives off a red glow due to its structural make-up and it is even said to burn hotter than most other types.

The Sirians themselves are very large, bi-pedal beings, most standing at least eight feet tall and some reaching a height of twelve feet or more. They are powerfully built with brown to gray skin and little hair on their body except for the top of their head which usually is pulled into a pony tail. Also a thin stripe of hair descends from that pony tail down their neck and back thinning out before the buttocks. They are a race of purely of conflict and breed every offspring as a warrior with one purpose, to fight. They are one of the most powerful and imperialistic governments in the Universe and they've been the cause to the extinction of many races.

Brutus stares ahead with Mace, "Um would you say that's a Sirian Starship Sergeant?"

Mace answers before the stunned expression can leave his face, "I would".

"Well what exactly is it doing here?", Brutus frantically asks. "I don't know" Mace replies, "but their sure not gonna identify us as friendly, we need to get outta here if we ever wanna find out."

Brutus is in the midst of saying, "I'm with ya there buddy" when out of nowhere their ship is hit by a preliminary barrage of Sirian fire. Red plasma rips through the fighter knocking out one of their engines and all hydraulics. Mace can barely keep control of the ship and couldn't land now even if they somehow made it to safety. A small Sirian fleet of fighters has emerged directly behind the UO ship. They do not continue to attack Mace, instead the ships surround him, flying in tight formation that essentially detains the UO vessel. The Sirians begin signaling to Mace with lights and radio bursts ordering him to follow them to the starship. Mace sees a dozen fighters on his radus monitor and knows he and Brutus have almost no chance of surviving an altercation with this fleet.

He looks to his friend and says, "Well, if they wanted to kill us they likely would have done it already."

Brutus gives him a discouraged look, "I'm sure the Sirian scum want to kill us, they probably just wanna find out what we're doing here first."

Mace shakes his head in agreement and seems to become engrossed in thought, "They obviously didn't wanna be discovered here, that's why they were on us so fast. This may be exactly the break our investigation needs. Narel and the Sirians have always been proposed allies, one of the few strong races whose ideals are somewhat aligned to his, it would make perfect sense.
We need to find out what they're up to."

Mace adjusts his trajectory to follow the Sirian flight path and sits back, still deep in thought.

Brutus soon replies, "We're the only ship out here and we have no back-up. We'll be dead before we ever set foot on this planet, how is that a break?"

Mace snaps out of his trance and smiles, "Cause sometimes my friend, things just come together. Our new mission is to get onto that planet and I know how we're gonna do it. This ship that good old Major Parra gave us is old, happens to be a class d-9 as a matter of fact."

Brutus cuts in, "So what, even less of a reason to go against those fighters."

Mace replies, "The only reason I remember them is because my dad used to talk about that model all the time back on Mars. He would always tell us how his d-9 was the greatest ship ever made. The best part about it he always bragged, was the hull. The alloys were molded in such a way that it was practically indestructible. He said that all three times he was shot down in one of these, the engines exploded with devastating force. The pressure would begin to build in the engine casings and the instruments would max out, that's how he knew when to release the engine from the ship. The blast would come moments later and was so powerful that the enemy always thought you were dead instantly, hence ending their pursuit. He would then perform what he called a comet landing by steering himself into the planet. That part I'm not happy about."

"This would be the time you decide to follow in your father's footsteps." Brutus cockily replies, "Are you sure the hull will be strong enough to protect us from the blast?"

"I can land us Brutus, just strap in" Mace says.

"Oh yea, act like I'm being negative, comet landing was real reassuring. I'm pretty sure comets land with a huge, planet smashing impact, not exactly your textbook escape tactic." Brutus mockingly replies as he straps himself into the cockpit.

Their ship gets closer and closer to the large, deep orange planet. Silver and brown veins run throughout the surface, signifying large deposits of ore and minerals. Mace does not know what the elemental make-up of the atmosphere is, but a deep orange color like this is usually caused by heavy concentrations of neon. Mace is careful to follow his escort's exact path. He plans to stay with the dozen Sirian fighters until the last possible moment. They are less than a few thousand yards from the gigantic overshadowing starship that dwarfs their petty fighter when two long, mechanical arms protrude from the mammoth craft. These arms are designed to capture an enemy vessel outside of the starship and investigate it for weapons and explosives before bringing it aboard. The Sirians have been a major target for suicide attacks over the centuries due to their imperialistic ways; this has led to a need for increased security measures such as this.

Mace watches patiently as the arms begin to move towards their ship. When they close in, the small fleet of Sirian fighters begin to back off slowly. As soon as they're clear, Mace launches his horizontal thrusters and spins his fighter just past the reach of the starship's outstretched arms. He now proceeds to open fire several times as he makes his escape, launching missiles and automated plasma turrets to attack as well as confuse. The unexpected assault eliminates three of the Sirian Fighters and creates a small cushion between the UO ship and it's pursuers. He now quickly maneuvers the ship downward, barreling towards the planet on only his thrusters until he abruptly fires their one good engine back up. Flying with the lone engine causes them to leave a thick smoke trail in their wake. Two new Sirian fighters approach from the front and Brutus takes care of them with the plasma turret. This does not deter the rest of the squadron behind them however, as they race to catch Mace while propelling towards the planet faster and faster. Mace pushes his remaining engine to full throttle attempting to get some more distance between him and the group. Even still, the relentless Sirians keep right on him and continue to gain ground as they plummet through the outer atmosphere. They fire a barrage of plasma rounds, but the UO fighter is still just out of their target range.

The Sirian Admiral quickly grows tired of the chase and orders all fighters that are equipped with missiles to launch all that they have. Over twenty high-explosive ship to ship PER-120 missiles are released towards the UO fighter just as it breaches the planet's inner atmosphere. This act couldn't come at a better time for the UO pair because shortly after the barrage is released the bombardment of missiles simultaneously detonates when colliding with the superheated barrier of one of Kutchatar's atmospheric boundaries. The Sirian fighters behind them are forced to back off in order to avoid their own explosion, but they manage to stay within both visual and radus range. They all successfully escape the blast, diverging and reconfiguring to quickly jump back onto Mace's trail. The UO fighter is now only about thirty seconds from hitting the planet's surface when the engine casings begin to go and Mace prepares to release them both. At this point he can no longer control the craft, the solider simply tries his best to guide the ship towards a soft- looking mountainside. He can see numerous hollow points and caverns across the hill face; this gives him hope that the terrain will somewhat cushion their landing. The engines are then released and detonate in their wake moments later, just as planned. The massive discharge gives the UO fighter an extra push as it crashes into the mountainside; showing Mace and Brutus first hand just why Mr. Crimson called it a comet landing. The Sirian ships above watch the large explosions and are convinced that the craft is destroyed. One Sirian officer, the squadron leader still decides to take his ship down just to be sure there are no survivors. He flies right over the mountainside where Mace and Brutus had crashed only moments before, oblivious to their presence. The entrance hole where they slammed into the planet blends in perfectly with the dozens of other tunnels sprouting up throughout the low-lying mountain range.

The landing itself is rough, but the rugged d-9 keeps the soldiers protected from a majority of the impact. Still, both Mace and Brutus are unconscious after the landing and Brutus awakens first, coming to while slumped forward with his seat-belt still holding tightly within the tail section of the fighter. He doesn't know if his friend is even conscious, but he speaks out anyway happy to be alive. "Well I have to give it to your dad, they sure don't build em like they used to!"

Brutus un-straps himself and rushes over to Mace who has a large knot on the side of his head from some debris that pierced the windshield just before impact. Mace is conscious, but a little woozy. Brutus helps him out of the cockpit and away from the ship. He lies his friend on the ground and gives him a supply pack to rest his head on before leaning back against a nearby rock.

Both of them try to regain themselves, "So what do ya think they did to pilots they didn't like, just forget to warn them about the nuclear engines", says Brutus sarcastically.

Mace laughs, "Or forget to tell them where the engine release is."

They both continue to laugh for a bit, temporarily relieved as it seems they've alluded the Sirians for now. While Brutus sits back against the cave wall he glimpses a shadow of something scurrying around the cave. He hops up and walks over to the decrepit ship where he grabs a light from their survival supplies. He shines it around the seemingly empty cave and can reveal nothing.

Mace gets up gingerly and tells Brutus, "We need to find out where to go from here."

"I thought you had a plan for that" says Brutus as he continues to shine his light around the large cavern.

Mace thinks for a moment then looks over to Brutus, "I might, did you see smoke when we were coming in?"

Brutus answers, "Obviously, our ship was on fire".

Mace replies, "No not from us, on the ground."

Brutus cockily responds, "Well no, I was kind of distracted".

"Well I saw at least half a dozen smoke stacks and as we both know, no Sirian technology would still use smoke emissions. That means there must be some sort of native civilized life of this planet. Wait, that bump to the head must have really got me, I remember the analysis of the planet before the crash and there is a primitive race here."

Brutus replies, "If their primitive, odds are they've been eradicated or enslaved by now so I doubt we can rely on the natives."

As he says this some more rustling can be heard from the rocks surrounding them. The two soldiers look to each other as now both of them hear the noise. Brutus lifts up his light again and shines it around the cavern once more. This time Mace can see a small figure jump behind one of the larger rocks as it's briefly illuminated. He picks up a plasma staff and slowly approaches the boulder. Brutus grabs one as well and moves in behind Mace to box the creature in.

The two are about to pounce on the intruder when a small figure, no more than three feet tall emerges from behind the rock quivering in fear.

"Haven't you done enough invaders, we've given in to all your demands." The little being pleads to them with genuine fear in his eyes.

He is a small creature with large ears and no apparent nose. His skin appears to change colors in order to blend in with his surroundings which happen to be the metallic silver rock of the cave walls at the present moment. Mace's information about a somewhat civilized species seems to be correct as this little creature is fully clothed and speaks the Versal language quite well. Mace and Brutus put down their plasma staffs and back off of him.

Mace says, "You have no reason to fear us. What race are you little friend?"

He looks up to them defiantly although still shaking, "Don't pretend to be my friend, I can't help but fear you because I've seen what you do. If you're going to kill me get it over with, don't insult me anymore."

Brutus replies, "You have no reason to fear us, honestly."

The tiny critter snaps back, "Why not! The rest of your people won't stop until my whole race is destroyed. You invaders want us all dead!"

Mace speaks softly to calm the little creature, "We're soldiers of the Universal Order, not invaders, you can trust us. Now who wants you dead, the beings occupying your planet now?"

The creature looks back to Mace seeming to relax somewhat, "Yes, them…but the first group came in peace, like you are now. They did not look like these large, evil beasts we see today. Some of the first travelers looked like you and some were even stranger. They told us that they were going to help move our people into a new age, with them as our divine allies."

Mace wonders who this first group of visitors were, "So the race that's here now, they weren't the first to come?"

He answers, "No, no the first group was made up of all different beings. As I said, most of them were more like your size and they didn't seem violent at all. I can't remember what they called themselves….oh yea, UAIR. I never found out what the name meant, but it was on all the boxes and supplies they brought down to the planet. They showed up a few years ago and discovered resources here that we didn't even know we had. UAIR began to bring supplies and educated my race on how to use the resources that had been naturally provided by our planet. We learned how to mine and purify everything from iron to platinum. They even taught us the Versal language, to move my people into more civilized communications.

Then, after the mines were established everything changed. They seemed to stop bringing supplies and began to only take them. Our leader was told that he must reimburse UAIR for their services, but as time went on they just continued to take. We thought that was bad, then about a week ago UAIR clears out and these creatures show up. They immediately brang destruction to our homes and stole every resource and supply they could find. We have nothing now. Most of our villages are already in ruins and they'll probably take Valeena by the end of the week. Even if my race makes it through this, our planet may be beyond repair. These new invaders are so cruel and empty hearted, I can't even believe there are species like them. I was in Galla, at my brother's house on the day they arrived. It was one of the earliest towns they seized and they had taken it within one day of setting foot on Kutchatar.

First, they sent in a small unit of soldiers that asked to borrow some minor supplies and fuel. Then, while the townspeople were helping them out, the Draka Scum takes inventory of what your town has. Later on, they return in much heavier numbers and take the supplies, leaving the people for dead without a single

resource….if they don't burn the town to the ground altogether.
Galla was spared, but I can name over a dozen that burned to ashes."

Mace feels for the little creature and is not at all surprised that the Sirians would be involved in something like this, "Don't worry my little friend we are from a different group of people; one that bands together all the races of the Universe. We didn't know about the plight of your planet until now, and we're not going to allow it I promise you that. You mentioned Valeena, is that your Capitol?"

The little being replies, "Yes, and if they destroy Valeena the morale of my people will never be restored. For some reason you bring me hope new visitor, but if you are not a member of those evil beasts they will surely kill you."

"That's why we don't plan on being seen, can you help us navigate the terrain?"

"Of course", responds the being, "I never did properly greet you. My name is Collo and my people are known as the Midians. We will be forever grateful if you could help us get back what's left of our home."

Mace says, "We'll do everything we can to get your freedom back, but first I need to contact my people, how long will it take us to get to Valeena?"

"Not long if you can keep up" says the little Midian, "Follow me".

"Thank you" replies Mace, "Let us grab our supplies and we'll be along."

Mace and Brutus walk back over to their ship.

Brutus looks to Mace and says, "What in the Verse could bring the Sirians here?"

"Didn't you hear? The planet is teeming with precious metals. My question is, who was here before them?"

Brutus replies, "Even if we could get through to the UO, we both know they wouldn't attack the Sirians over this. So what's the plan once we get to Valeena?"

Mace smiles, "Save the innocent and punish the wicked".

Brutus grabs his arm, "Remember we have a bigger mission right now, don't go and try to save this world. It's not our job."

Mace pulls his arm from Brutus' grip, "Like you said; we can't get in contact with the Order and we need to get off this planet to continue our mission. If you didn't notice, that happens to be a Sirian Starship out there. Right next to it sits another half a dozen warships and at least one cruiser so I think we're gonna need a pretty big distraction to get off this orange rock. Therefore, if saving these beings goes hand in hand with our mission who are you to intervene?"

Brutus sighs, then he and Mace walk back to Collo.

Mace looks over to the tiny Midian, "So how exactly can we get to Valeena without being seen by Sirian Patrols?"

Collo laughs and replies, "Do you think those overgrown barbarians can even fit through most of these caves? Our caverns run almost all the way across Kutchatar, how do ya think we've survived this long? The one thing you need to remember is that an echo can travel for miles through here, so we need to stay quiet during the journey."

Collo begins to lead them down one of the caverns as Mace and Brutus look around at how many paths there truly are. Dozens, if not hundreds of tunnels intersect at the few junctions where the cave opens up. Carved intricately out of metallic rock, the cave walls look magnificent in the few places where light shines freely. It amazes Mace that such a primitive being can master such a complex tunnel system, but thats the advantage of being at home, nobody knows it better than you.

The three remain quiet as they make their way, sometimes crossing over flowing streams of bromine along with other toxic liquids and even open cliffsides blanketed in darkness. With the combination of environmental dangers and lack of light within these tunnels, Mace and Brutus are both more than appreciative to have their guide.

After nearly an hour they come to an underpass where a decent sized regiment of Sirian troops are marching directly overtop of their heads. They can also hear rain pouring down as they allow the troops to pass, but even once their gone Collo still holds the UO soldiers in place.

He explains, "This is one of the only sections of our tunnels that cut off. There is a large concentration of platinum just up ahead, and I'm sure you know we can't drill through that. We're just gonna have to make a run across the field above it, after we pass the main quarry the tunnels open up again."

As they come out of the caverns Mace and Brutus look across a massive field of silver tipped bushes. Even in the darkness these bushes reflect a silver glow and Collo begins to explain what they're looking at.

"Mercundrum are bushes with sharp thorns that grow above the metal deposits on the surface of our planet. They are quite flexible under normal conditions, but when damaged they release a thick, metallic sap that hardens to repair and protect the plant. The sap dries to be as sharp as your spears and as strong as your armor I assure you that."

"So what happened to these?" asks Brutus.

Collo replies, "The invaders trampled the fields with their convoys and war machines. Most if not all of these mercundrum are dead, encased within their dried sap. This makes the path very dangerous, but still we must be quick and thorough, do you think you can keep up?"

Mace says, "We'll get through, just lead the way."

"Good" says Collo, "it doesn't really matter how we get there, just as long as we make it to the main cave on the other side without being spotted." Collo points to a narrow opening that can barely be seen across the lengthy field.

"Now let's go, the quicker the better."

Brutus mocks, "Right, make a run for it. That had to be at least a legion that just passed over our heads."

Mace says, "We have no choice, we have to go."

Before Brutus can even refute any further, Mace and then Collo storm out of the Cave running like prisoners in a jail break. Collo runs nearly uninhibited, as most of the Mercundrum branches stretch out above his head. Mace and Brutus are not so lucky, the sharp branches latch on and scrape underneath their armor. They are forced to slow down as the faster they move the more caught up and entangled they become. The limbs are razor sharp and the metal surface surrounding the core plant is very thick. As they slow up Mace begins to take notice of the horizon. He can see a litter of Sirian watchtowers and a pair of fortresses being built in the distance; the Barbaric race was indeed smothering this planet with their occupation. They wanted Kutchatar's materials for something and they wanted them bad.

The brush becomes more condensed as they move along and some areas have Mercundrum bushes tangled together into large masses stretching twenty or more feet into the air. Collo is long gone by now, but Mace tries to reassure Brutus, "We know where he's going, we can take our time and meet him on the other side".

Brutus says, "I wouldn't be too sure of that, don't you remember the dwarf's farewell motto, the quicker the better? We might be in trouble here buddy."

Mace says, "Relax, looks like the Sirians are still setting up, they probably don't even have local patrols out yet. Besides how can you even patrol this stuff? A Sirians oversized body can't exactly step right through, we'll see em comin from a mile away."

The two continue on slowly but surely as the rain helps shields their movements, unfortunately it also makes the already hazardous field very slippery. The duo attempts to stay confident as they pass an abandoned mining drill that just about marks the halfway point of the wretched fields. They pause for a moment as a faint noise can now be heard through the rain. Brutus and Mace both look to the sky. They then glance back to each other and attempt to move a bit further when a vibrant light shines down from above. The light is intended to blind the two, but the reflection glaring back off the metallic bushes is so luminous that the ship above is temporarily blinded and begin to fire aimlessly into the field. Mace and Brutus now disregard their bodies and the bushes around them; they begin storming through the field as if nothing were in their way. The ship above shuts off the blinding light and Mace looks back to see that it's some new model of Sirian Patrol craft. It's got a small hull and four hover engines that allow for quick maneuvering. Plasma cannons and turrets hang out all over the ship as it's engines twist and turn to re-adjust. The Sirian pilots switch their visual over to infrared which takes the glare off the field and exposes the two soldiers from cover. The ship quickly re-engages the targets and begins firing at will, raining plasma down onto the field once more.

Mace yells out to Brutus, "Follow me!"

The two turn and cut across the field drastically, now heading for a large entanglement of Mercundrum that stands about thirty feet away from them. The Sirian Patrol Ship flies past them after the duo's quick change of direction, but again quickly repositions itself and continues the chase. Just as it reaches full speed again the UO team reaches the massive Mercundrum patch.

Mace yells to Brutus, "down, now!"

The two of them duck and roll underneath the massive knot of bushes. Due to the infrared switch, the Patrol Ship is blind to the brush at this point and they clip a long protrusion extending from the Mercundrum patch. The strong Mercundrum branches puncture the Sirian ship, breeching numerous areas and causing significant damage. Debris drops all around Mace and Brutus as the Sirians lose an engine and a good portion off the back of their ship. They try to save it and regain command, but spin out of control as they hover off into the distance. Mace and Brutus seem relieved for a moment, but as it disappears they see two ejections shoot from the top of the ship.

Brutus says, "Drop pods, think we can make it?"

Mace doesn't even look to the end of the field which is still at least a hundred yards away. "No, don't move."

The two sit in silence as the two pods land not far from them, in the opposite direction of where they're headed. Mace signals Brutus to proceed slowly and the two begin to do so, keeping their focus on the Sirian's drop point. They push aside the Mercundrum plants ever so cautiously, but the metal limbs still chime and cling together with every movement. Additional rustling can be heard following frantically behind them and shortly after starting Mace says, "Wait."

The two stop again and Brutus grabs his plasma staff and begins to take it off his back. Mace shakes his head no as he points to the Mercundrums. Using a plasma staff with these bushes around would probably mean certain death for both parties. Instead Mace clutches his CIR and Brutus follows suit. It is silent again, and the UO pair is still unsure of exactly where the Sirians are.

The silence is broken by some movement coming from behind them, somewhere in between their position and the end of the field. The noise comes from the opposite side of where the Sirian pods dropped in. Brutus turns to look, but it must have just been a distraction because as soon as he does the two Sirians begin to rush the soldiers from the front firing a barrage of plasma along the way. The red plasma cartridges are ripped apart by the Mercundrum limbs and none of the liquid quite makes it to Mace and Brutus. The two fire back for a moment, but then hastily continue to run as the Sirians relentlessly gain ground. Fighting a warrior race with the size and strength of the Sirians in close quarters on a field this treacherous would be sheer suicide.

"Run little cowards, run!" shouts one of the ruthless monsters as they march relentlessly through their own plasma which remains burning atop the Mercundrum branches. Their skin is scorched and scraped, yet it barely delays them. Mace and Brutus try to pick up the pace, but the dagger-like branches are becoming too much for them. Mace realizes that something must be done. He swings his CIR over his shoulder and shouts over to his friend, "No matter what, keep going!"

Mace then turns course slightly, grabs onto one of the larger Mercundrum plants, and swings himself up onto a fairly high branch. He's careful to avoid the six inch protruding thorns present on this particular shrub, thorns that are more like metal spikes at this point. He maneuvers into a stable position and from his perch Mace gets his first clear look at the soldier that's chasing him. He takes aim and fires several times before the Sirian can get a shot on him. The plasma rounds hit inside the Mercundrums in front of his enemy, but they splatter close enough that the Sirian is sprayed nearly head to toe with plasma. The beast yells in pain and Mace sees an open shot just above his neck plate. He takes it and the miraculous shot weaves through the Mercundrums and hits the target right through the neck, killing him instantly. The second Sirian soldier, who was previously chasing Brutus witnesses this and now has a clear look at Mace sitting in such an elevated and exposed position. Brutus sees this as well and as the Sirian lines up he begins firing at will to cover for his friend. The Sirian is not hit by Brutus, but he is quite distracted and Mace is able to reposition himself on the branch. The last Sirian turns back to Brutus and Mace delivers a second kill shot, this one also goes straight through the neck, just above the armor plate. The Sirian falls to the ground and Mace drops down from the branch to regroup with his friend.

"Good work" he says as he pushes his way through more Mercundrums, "Now let's get outta here before any more show up."

The two are now only about fifty yards from the exit and they successfully proceed to the end without further incident. Thankfully, Collo is waiting for them at the tunnel entrance which is again at a junction of numerous different sized caverns.

"Wow, I guess you really are Universal Protectors I've never seen anyone defeat the invaders before" says Collo anxiously as is he surprised to see his new friends emerge from the skirmish he just witnessed.

Mace replies, "They're far from defeated little friend. Now are we almost there?"

Collo tells them, "Yea, this one leads straight to Valeena, not much longer at all."

He points down the largest tunnel within the junction and they continue on their way. After another hour or so Collo proclaims, "It's just ahead."

As Mace and Brutus turn the final corner within the long passageway they can see it open up into the Capitol City. They are now looking at the underlevels of Valeena, here thousands of Midian soldiers and laborers can be seen working on everything from farming equipment to low grade weapons.

Collo is excited to be home and he runs ahead waving them along, "Follow me, I'll take you to the resistance organizer, Keila. We didn't have a military before we were attacked and she started the first militia to resist the invaders. We haven't had much…well any success yet, but like you she does give me hope."

As they walk through Valeena Mace and Brutus see the basic yet vast network of Midian life. Their homes and buildings are constructed from some sort of dried clay that appears to be quite durable. Most houses are crammed together side by side and make-shift dwellings were also standing everywhere except the road. These smaller, more ramshackle huts are composed mostly of cut trees and wire. The people are packed in extremely tight; the living situation is perceived by both soldiers as being dangerously dense. It seems as though Collo was right, most of what's left of the Midian people have been packed into this one, last standing city. As they continue to walk, the group ascends up several long ramps that access the various levels of the capitol. Near the top, Mace is surprised to see the land clear up. There was neither housing, nor buildings on the upper levels, only farmland and the skies above. Valeena was nestled nicely inside a small valley within a mountain. There appeared to be only two ways in; a bridge on the top level of Valeena, at the front where there was a break in the mountainside surrounding the city, and the tunnel systems leading to the levels below.

Collo yells out, "There she is" and walks them right up to a group of Midians who seem to be deep in discussion.

Two of the less than four foot tall Midian guards step in front of Mace and Brutus, creating a barrier between them and Keila. Brutus snickers at the idea that these two little beings think they could hold the soldiers back.

Mace is much more polite and says, "Hello, we're from the Universal Order, protectors of the Universe and all its inhabitants, I'm Mace and this is Brutus."

"Really", Keila snidely responds, "well I must thank you for all your protection thus far."

Mace pauses for a moment, then humbly replies, "We apologize for not bringing aid sooner, but we've only just learned of your situation and now we're here to help."

Keila is not convinced, "How do we know you're not with the invaders?"

Brutus laughs openly and says, "Would they really need to use espionage? Seems like rolling up to your doorstep trumpets blaring has been working fairly well."

She doesn't find him amusing, but reluctantly agrees, "I guess your right, besides you do seem much more civilized than those beasts. So what is it you think can you do, we're having enough trouble trying to protect this city we can't even begin to worry about getting our planet back. Where is the rest of your support anyway, this is no task for a pair of soldiers."

Mace replies, "We don't have any support yet, but with your help we can still save this city. I'm not sure how much time we have, but if you'll take my friend Brutus here to retrieve the parts we need to restore our ship, I'll help you formulate a plan that'll save this refuge."

Keila thinks for a second then says, "How do I know you won't just stall until he repairs your ship, then leave us all?"

"Because", Mace replies, "you're going to be attacked before he can even fix our ship. I've battled this enemy before. The Sirian lines I observed on our way in are already setting this planet up as a stronghold of some sort, they have you completely boxed in. I'm surprised they haven't laid ruin to this city already."

Keila lets out a frustrated sigh before giving in, she knows that as of right now her people are doomed. She's far too desperate to turn away any possible help. "Fine, we're not a very aeronautically advanced race, however we do produce many different components for other species. We have a small depot on the third level with those and other parts we've salvaged over time. Several of Keila's people take Brutus to retrieve the parts for their ship."

Mace now says to Keila, "Ok, so Collo has already described the Sirians' recent method of siege to me. Now they're usually pretty straightforward with their tactical procedures so I doubt they'll stray from that same approach as long as they haven't received too much resistance."

Keila replies, "No, all of our other cities were much more vulnerable, I doubt there was any resistance at all. A vast majority of our people abandoned their homes and have fallen back to Valeena for a reason. Our Capitol has never been taken in the sixteen centuries of recorded Midian Civilization and my people keep faith that it will continue to stand. This is also the only city with a missile shield, although I doubt we'll even need it. I had thought before that it was the one good thing we got from UAIR, but this enemy hasn't used a single missile on us."

Mace replies, "Not yet, still its a good thing to have. It will halt any attack from the sky, not just missiles. It actually really helps us that you haven't resisted in any other cities; it means they shouldn't be expecting much of a fight here. Have they sent in a scout team yet?"

"No", she says, "Nothing yet".

"I'll be right back" says Mace, just before he walks over and begins climbing a watch tower that is just a few yards from where the two were talking. Being surrounded by a mountain range, it is a good climb to the top of the tower. Since they're currently on the highest level of Valeena, he can see far out across the vast plains of Kutchatar. He climbs up about sixty feet, then looks out to the horizon where numerous Sirian defense posts and fortresses can be seen looming in the distance. A cruiser and several starships can also be seen as Mace looks to the sky above. He then takes note of the mountain surrounding the city, it is a treacherous rock formation on a very defensive position, he can understand why the city has never been captured. He still only sees one viable entrance to Valeena; a large, stone bridge that passes over a steep canyon at a lone break in the mountain, stretching no more than seventy yards long and thirty yards across. All but this small section of the city's borders appear to be secure and unsurpassable by Sirian ground vehicles. Mace is pleased by this geographical advantage and quickly climbs down from the post."

He says to Keila, "Other than the tunnel system, is that bridge the only way in or out of this City?"

She responds, "Yes, why?"

Mace happily replies, "Don't you see, if we disable that bridge the Sirians most likely will abandon their attempt. The effort that it will take them to seize the city with no entrance and a missile shield will far outweigh the bounty they'll receive from taking it. It's so simple."

"Disable it, how?" Responds Keila.

"We'd have to destroy" Mace answers, "it's the only way to be sure it'll keep em out."

Keila jumps back in, "No, that's not an option!"

Shocked, Mace refutes, "Why, not?"

"Because we need that bridge, we can't nearly fit a majority of our farming and mining equipment through the tunnel system. If we blow the bridge we'll be cut off from all our resources. There are thousands of Midians living in Valeena now and we don't have nearly enough food growing within these walls. Not to mention the moral defeat that losing it would mean to the people. The Bridge of Valeena is the first large-scale structure we'd ever completed and it's stood strong for over six centuries. So I'll say again, that's not an option."

Mace, now frustrated responds, "It's the only option. Lose the bridge or lose your lives."

He walks away as Keila struggles with the incredible dilemma that's been put in front of her. Destroy the bridge now and she avoids conflict with the Sirians, but who knows how many people will die in the months to come as food rations drop and drop. She's in an impossible spot and can see no right choice, but she refuses to choose a solution which will indefinitely endanger her people.

Mace sees that Brutus has returned from the Midian storage houses. Brutus walks up to him with several bags of supplies on his shoulder and a couple of Midian workers trailing him who are carrying some additional bags full of greasy tools and parts.

"They didn't have a lot of direct matches for our parts, but I should be able to salvage what we need from these other components."

"Good", Mace replies, "get the ship ready to go as soon as you can."

While Brutus and Mace converse, a look-out standing atop one of the Midian watch towers frantically yells out, "Invaders approaching! Invaders approaching!"

Mace looks across the bridge to the horizon and sees a small party of Sirians moving in on two of their high-speed ground craft. Sirian ground vehicles range in size and shape, but like many militaries these days they mostly use powerful hovering technologies to propel and control their craft. This allows armies to glide across the various types of terrain throughout the Verse friction free. Sirian vehicles all have plasma turrets mounted on their bows, turrets that can devastate a town like this. Many also have plasma cannons or additional tactical weaponry placed in custom positions. They are approaching extremely fast, but the fortress they've been deployed from is a good distance away so there's still a few minutes before they'll arrive.

Mace turns back to Brutus, "Did you happen to see the Midian weapon supplies?"

Brutus pauses a second, "Yea or should I say lack of a supply; they might as well fight with sticks and stones against the Sirians."

"What about explosives?" Mace asks.

Brutus thinks hard, "I saw a few timing mines and some blast blocks, but that's it. I don't think that'll be a problem though if that's what they need."

Mace responds, "Yea why not?"

"Cause they do have a ten civilization supply of fertilizer down there, we could build enough XC-20 to blow a moon off this planet."

Mace begins walking up to the Bridge of Valeena in order to get a better look at the point where he'll most likely engage the enemy. He walks about halfway across the sturdy, well-built bridge which stretches far into the deep canyon below. It was only about a half mile from one end of the canyon to the other, but the depths it stretched to were incredible with the bottom seeming nonexistent; vanishing into infinite darkness. The structure of the bridge itself was quite impressive, supported by a massive pillar of the strange dried clay.

This sole support beam was bent and hardened across the massive crevice, lying like a boomerang fused to each canyon wall. To most Versalized races this structure would seem medieval or obsolete, but to a race on the Midian's societal and technological levels it was a modern marvel. With the current conditions on Kutchatar both UO soldiers realize that it would be impossible to rebuild this wonder. Mace continues walking to the end of the bridge and peers out at the advancing scout party of Sirian soldiers. When he reaches the end, Mace notices that just in front of the bridge mouth, where the road has been worn down over time there is about a six foot deep trench that leads into the plains and thick foliage surrounding the mountainside. The eroded trench extends around a thirty to forty yard curve leading away from the bridge. Mace follows the curve of the road to see that the trench continues for another fifty yards or so at a slightly shorter depth of four and a half feet before tapering off in the open terrain. As the Sirians cross the plains they will simply hover through this trench just before crossing the bridge to take Valeena.

Mace turns to Brutus and yells, "Do we have any auto-turrets?"

He walks toward Mace and responds, "Actually, I saw an old one in the Midian warehouse, looked like it was still in working condition."

Mace stares across the ground at the mouth of the bridge, he then makes several measurements with his feet before marking a thick tree a few yards away from the front of the bridge.

He yells over to Brutus once more, "Set the auto-turret up with its sight aimed to exactly that mark. Then I need you to take a CIR with zoom and set up on the left side of the bridge. Make sure you're far enough out of sight that they can't point you out."

Brutus sighs, "What do you plan to do, we're not even prepared to fight this basic detachment."

Mace replies, "I know, we're just buying some time right now, trust me. Watch for my signal, right arm you fire the auto, left arm you shoot straight through a helmet. Just make sure it's not mine."

Brutus smiles, "I'll try" he says, as he hurries off to set up the turret.

Mace now turns to Keila who's followed him onto the bridge, "They'll be here in five or six minutes, I need your best trained soldiers standing on this bridge in four."

She replies, "Not a problem" and hurries off to gather them.

These five minutes pass quickly, but Keila manages to pack the bridge with a convincing number of armed Midians. As they close in, Mace identifies the Sirian vehicles, they are a fairly common design known as turriots. These small, bi-level hovercrafts require a driver on the bottom level and between two and four manned turrets on the elevated second level.

Mace stands at the front of the bridge as the small Sirian convoy, carrying less than a dozen soldiers, approaches Valeena without caution. The beastly Sirians, who stand at an average height of eight feet tall laugh and mock the Midians who defend the bridge, further ridiculing the race they endanger and exploit. Their dry, pale brown skin is rough and callous, while their most distinguishing feature is undoubtedly a long, thin strip of hair starting on their lower back and extending all the way up into a pony tail atop the center of their scalp. The rest of their oversized bodies are hairless with three toes on each foot and four fingers on each hand. The disgusting Sirian infantrymen have dried blood and guts stuck to their armor, with untended wounds and scars on nearly every one of them.

They advance right up to Mace before stopping their vehicles just a few feet from the Midian lines. The Sirians park their turriots one behind the other and step down from their positions to confront the enemy. A Lieutenant leads the way, marching until he's face to face with Sergeant Crimson. His eleven soldiers slowly line up next to him, staring at the Midian people like Valeena was some sort of restaurant and they hadn't eaten in years.

The Lieutenant stares coldly at Mace, "What business does the UO have on this planet?"

Mace replies, "I could ask you the same, but my Commander told me to wait until he got here to ask questions."

The Sirian remarks, "We're doing no wrong, our army is using Kutchatar as a medical depot during the war. We have been plagued by heavy casualties and seek assistance; our only reason for this visit today is to borrow supplies. Just a few meds and we'll be on our way…the Sirian Army guarantees they'll be reimbursed of course."

Mace replies, "Oh is that what happened to the rest of this planet, were you looking for supplies? You seem to have a funny way of collecting meds, not sure I agree with it friend."

The Sirian ignites his sye and Mace simultaneously ignites his staff, but neither soldier strikes.

The Sirian furiously shouts, "This planet was plagued when we arrived and before that it was never more than a spot on the map. This feeble race means nothing and one UO soldier is not enough to stop me from carrying out my orders. Now are you going to let us check for supplies or do we have to send a message?"

The other Sirian soldiers now ignite their syes as well.

Mace smiles in the Sirian's face, "Who said I was alone? I have a line of snipers set up just behind this bridge and as we both know, UO snipers are very accurate."

The Sirian's expression seems unconvinced.

"Do you believe me?" asks Mace after a slight pause.

The Sirian smuggly replies, "No" and Mace raises his right hand signaling Brutus to trigger the auto-turret.

He does so and the turret fires a plasma round that zips past the Sirian line, missing one of them by only a few inches before smashing into the tree Mace had marked out earlier.

The Sirian Lieutenant says, "Not very precise is he?"

"That was your warning shot." Mace responds, "You know the UO and their rules, but I can see that you need something a bit more convincing."

Mace now lifts his left arm and from his left side comes another plasma round, this one missing Mace's shoulder by mere inches before soaring right through one of the Sirians open helmets, killing him instantly. Brutus has targeted the soldier standing right next to the cocky Lieutenant, brains and blood from his fallen comrad spray onto the Sirian Officer as well as several others. The soldiers behind him all begin to lunge towards Mace.

Expecting the charge he yells out, "I have a whole line of em, touch me and they take every one of you out!"

The Lieutenant halts his soldiers and holds them off. "Fall Back", he shouts, "The Sirians angrily obey the order and halt, snorting and snarling in disgust. "Back to the barracks", barks the Lieutenant.

An evil smile seems to show that the officer is somewhat impressed as they slowly retreat to their turriots, "We'll be back you know…and no amount of snipers will hold us off."

The Sirians turn around and head back to their base. The Midians remain calm as their enemy leaves, then once the convoy is out of range they begin to joyfully celebrate as if they had just won a war. Mace makes his way through the triumphant crowd that engulfs the bridge, trying to move toward Brutus and Keila who stand just behind the madness.

When he finally does, Mace has a little grin on his face as he is happy for the Midians moral victory.

When he gets over to them Keila says, "What next?"

Mace takes a drink from a Midian fountain, "We let the people celebrate a while, then we clear the bridge so we can set our explosives. Tomorrow they'll be back, we need to be ready."

Mace then turns to head over to the supply warehouses and begin building the explosives, "Brutus meet me at the warehouse when you're ready, I'm gonna get started."

On his way Keila catches up to him, "I told you already, blowing up the bridge isn't an option."

Mace turns and replies, "Do you like this feeling?"

"What feeling?" She says.

"Victory, hope, relief?"

"Yea of course, Who wouldn't?"

He stops and looks her in the face, "Then just trust me from now on. I will save your people and preserve that bridge I give you my word. You're the leader here and I need your support, but my plan will work a lot better if I don't have to explain myself. So can you trust me?"

She looks over to the bridge where her people still continue to rejoice over the first moral victory they've had in months, "I can. Do what you have to do."

Mace replies, "Thank you" and follows Brutus down to the storage facilities where the Midian fertilizer supply is kept.

As they walk over Mace asks, "Do we have anything with nitro methane?"

Brutus replies, "I already tested their basic fuel, it's got triple the concentration we need."

Mace smiles, "Perfect".

The two get to the agricultural supply facility and Brutus turns on the dim lights to expose a warehouse full of farming equipment and supplies with fertilizer bales stacked in rows stretching as far as the eye can see. The soldiers gather some tools and begin their demolitions work, converting fertilizer into explosives like machines. They fill everything from small pales to fuel drums with a potent explosive mixture. After several hours of highly productive labor, they've created enough improvised munitions to destroy the bridge several times over.

Brutus says to Mace, "You know even if we do succeed tomorrow, once we get off this planet they're all doomed. They'll never be able to hold off the Sirians without us and you know the UO won't view the maltreatment of the Midian Race as being of Universal importance."

Mace replies, "I know, but I still can't sit here and do nothing. Besides, there's something not exactly right here. Nine times out of ten not even a regiment of UO troops would keep the Sirians out of a city they plan to siege. We should have had to kill those soldiers, even a small detachment of Sirians is usually far too headstrong to back down like that."

Brutus replies, "What do ya think it was?"

Mace responds, "I don't know, but I can't help thinking it has something to do with what they're doing here in the first place. Just think of how far this planet is from the Centaur-Sirian war, why would they ever need this for military reasons? There must be a few dozen high resource planets that would be much more accessible."

Brutus has no answer and simply shrugs his shoulders.

Mace looks down at all the explosives they've assembled, "This is more than enough. I'll set all the charges; you better get back to our ship. Even if you work on it through the night you may not be done by morning."

Brutus is happy to continue his repairs, "Oh I'll be done, I'm not dying on this planet tomorrow I can assure you of that."

Brutus makes his way back to the ship and Mace works through the night setting every charge that he and Brutus cooked up. He even got a few hours of rest before sunrise. On Kutchatar it was dark for only twelve hours out of a twenty eight hour day. At least one of their two nearest stars shined brightly for the remaining sixteen hours.

The Midians of Valeena get a good night's sleep and Keila won't begin awakening her soldiers until dawn. The previously demoralized race gets their first good rest in over a week, as every previous night had brought nothing but fear and worry. Often times, they wouldn't get to sleep at all as the Sirian machinery rumbling through the fields gets to be so loud that not even their leaders could tell if it were an invasion or not. Although things still look bleak for the troubled species, tonight they feel as though they can hold there heads up high and face the enemy with dignity and pride when morning breaks. The Midians have finally seen that their goliath-like adversary can be defeated, and like most beings they can even be intimidated. Tomorrow for this young species will truly be a new day, and one with much graver consequences.

As the first sun rises, so does Mace who checks in with all the guards posted atop Valeena's watch towers to make sure they hadn't seen anything overnight. He surveys the horizon himself and is then greeted by Brutus who has just returned from repairing the ship.

Mace, sounding shocked says, "I didn't expect to see you this early."

"You didn't think I was gonna miss this did ya?" Replies Brutus, who then pulls out a couple pairs of Visocs which he brought back from the ship. He hands one pair to his friend and takes the other for himself. They both walk up to the Bridge and check opposite sides of the horizon for any Sirian mobilization. The Visoc's microcomputer scans the distant terrain up to fifty miles away and zooms in on specific targets based on heat, movement, element, or various other programmable settings. Mace and Brutus both set their Visocs to target motion and after a few minutes Brutus spots something. He points the coordinates out to Mace who sets his to the same region. Mace can see that several Sirian Citadels are mobilizing troops for an upcoming assault. As they continue to watch, it becomes clear that all five fortresses visible on the horizon were preparing to attack Valeena. Mace summons Keila from her dwelling and directs all available Midian soldiers to take their positions on the bridge. Keila backs up this order and she along with her soldiers are soon ready and waiting for their final stand.

Today the Sirians use a much faster vehicle to approach the city. Their legions pack into troop transport vehicles called hyracs. These advanced personnel carriers float above the terrain on an electromagnetic cushion and propel themselves using small, water-based rocket engines. Each transport ship uses an open design, created strictly for use on the battlefield. This allows Sirian soldiers to readily jump out and fight after the target is reached. They can also bail from the transport if necessary to avoid high casualty amounts in the event the transport is shot down. The hyracs that Mace and Brutus encountered during the war usually held somewhere between one and three hundred Sirian soldiers. As this new Sirian convoy nears, Mace can see ten hyracs. From this, he knows he'll be dealing with at least a thousand of these vicious enemy beasts.

He and Brutus put away the Visocs and Mace tells Keila to pull back all of her people from the bridge.

Keila snaps back, "We need to defen..."

Mace cuts into her sentence, "We don't have time to argue, trust me Keila, remember?"

Keila sticks to her word and doesn't question the request any further. She gives the order and the rest of the Midian soldiers move to positions behind the bridge. Mace and Brutus walk to the mouth of the Midian superstructure where several detonators and cables can be seen draped across ground. Even at first glance, the bridge is noticeably wired.

Brutus says to him, "Looks good".

Mace responds, "I know. There's no reason for both of us to stay, there's nothing else you can do. If the city falls, get back to the ship and report everything to Lang."

Brutus shakes his head reluctantly and says, "Good luck buddy."

Brutus then walks back across the bridge and waits behind the Midian lines. The soldiers are so small that he can easily see over the crowd, giving him a clear view of his friend.

Mace stands alone on the bridge about ten feet from where it turns into the road. On that road, just a few thousands yards away, the battalion of Sirian warriors race toward him itching for a fight. Mace now pulls a thin, tube shaped metal detonator out of his armor that shines vibrantly in the morning light. He watches the overwhelming number of Sirians approach and stares the hyracs down adamantly as they close in.

Each transport ship looked to be the smaller model, only a few hundred feet long. Mace was relieved as this meant he would probably only be dealing with around a thousand Sirian soldiers as opposed to the three thousand that the larger hyracs would have brought. The hyrac line continues into the narrow gully leading up to the bridge, crumbling over trees and road markers that stand in their way. The entire convoy stops inside the trench-like road at the front of Valeena. They park one behind the other with the lead hyrac stopping less than a dozen feet from Mace. The Sirians begin to exit their vehicles when the Lieutenant who had been present the day before steps out and orders all soldiers to form lines behind a commander who is just exiting a hyrac himself. This head Sirian slides on his helmet as he begins to approach the bridge. It's clear this was a high ranking Commander due to numerous tech upgrades and dozens of commendation plates attached to his top tier armor, plates that were only given to acknowledge superior battlefield achievement and leadership. During all his time in the war, Mace had never encountered such a highly decorated member of the Sirian military.

Keila attempts to keep track of the forming enemy lines, but loses count quickly in the sea of soldiers that seems to keep growing, almost like a tide that had been at it's lowest and just keeps coming in. This is the first time that she realizes yesterday was a joke, they would need nothing short of a miracle to survive today. Most of the other Midians feel this reality dose as well and begin to tremble with fear. Even Brutus worries that these may be the last moments he will see his friend alive. Mace has gotten through plenty of tight situations, but this one would definitely take the cake.

The tension from almost every being inside Valeena was as thick as can be imagined, that's ALMOST every being. Mace however, stands confidently on the bridge as the Sirian commander halts his advancing lines. The commander continues up to Mace alone and walks out about five feet onto the mouth of the bridge.

Once he reaches this distance Mace proclaims, "That's far enough."

The Sirian laughs condescendingly and says, "Oh no human, this isn't nearly far enough. You see, we need to resupply and that requires us to move into the city, so that's exactly what we're gonna do."

Mace replies, "Well I've already inventoried this city for the UO and there's nothing here worth taking. So why don't you just move on?"

"Well my universal protector, I can't do that." Replies the Commander. "Truthfully, I don't even wanna do that. Especially when I know that UAIR sold this town plenty of supplies that we happen to find extremely useful. Now step aside and let us pass!"

Mace shouts defiantly, "The entire bridge is wired, move one step closer and I take it out."

The Commander does not seem convinced as his condescending laugh turns to a sadistic smile. "Do you think we're fools UO soldier? We know that this is the only multi-purpose entrance to the city. If you were to destroy this bridge it would keep us out, but it would also give what's left of this pathetic civilization a death sentence. That's not something I believe you'd do."

"Giving them a death sentence would be letting you by, now for the last time, fall back Commander!"

The Sirian Commander is undeterred and signals his men to advance across the bridge. Keila, Collo, and many other Midians cling together while cringing in fear as their dreaded nightmare of the invaders crossing into Valeena comes true right before their very eyes.

Mace holds up the detonator and squeezes it tight, staring the Commander down. Without any further hesitation he presses the button and quickly drops to the ground. Multiple large explosions begin to set off in unison; flames fill the air instantaneously and the shockwave alone knocks all bystanders to the ground. The bridge's support pillar is knocked off balance, causing the bridge to shake violently for nearly twenty seconds before finally restabilizing itself. The blast concussion was devastating and with so much smoke and debris it appeared to all that Mace was in fact forced to destroy the bridge in order to save them.

Beleaguered cries from stunned Midians can be heard from all angles as panic soon joins the smoke filled air. Midian Soldiers and spectators alike struggle to get to their feet and regain their bearing. The rumbling of the bridge has ceased and many fear that it lies at the bottom of the unfathomably deep canyon.

Suddenly, out of nowhere one of the lookouts shouts loudly, "The bridge is still here, it's still here!"

The fear turns to cheers as the people begin to see that this is true. As the air settles and visibility slowly returns it looks as though the bridge is still standing strong. Keila grabs the visocs Mace left behind and attempts to peer through the murky air. As she catches a glimpse across the bridge, the trench that led into Valeena has noticeably widened, in fact it had nearly tripled in size. Debris and rubble cover the ground and the smoke will take several more minutes to fully dissipate, but it looked as though the bridge has been preserved. Keila runs carelessly through the thick cloud, desperate to see what's become of Mace. She begins running out onto the bridge blindly, assuming that the fact the bridge looks to still be standing implies it's structural integrity also remains intact.

Brutus, who also anxiously awaits the fate of his friend attempts to stop her calling out, "Wait, we don't know it's safe yet! Any extra weight could cause a collapse!"

Standing at the mouth of the bridge he blocks her path, but the thrifty Midian turns on a dime and bolts right past him without the slightest delay.

Brutus says, "Great, I guess now everyone has a hero complex", just before sprinting out right behind her.

Luckily, the bridge appears to have shaken off the detonation and doesn't show any signs of significant damage; mostly just superficial cracks and deficiencies. It feels like they're running forever before Keila finally sees a massive body spread out near the front of the bridge, one far too large to be Mace. As she gets closer the shiny detonator can be seen, still clutched tightly within his hand, it was Mace.

She yells back to Brutus, who's now not very far behind, "I found him!"

The dead Sirian Commander lies atop his body when Brutus and Keila finally reach him. The two pull the Sirian carcass off of their friend and help him back to his feet. He remains a little stunned and hard of hearing, but smiles joyfully as he looks out at the devastated Sirian convoy.

As she hugs the soldier tight, Keila, ecstatic with excitement says, "You wired the road cause you knew they would try and cross the bridge. You're a genius and I love the Universal Order Mace Crimson. The Midians owe you our lives, thank you, thank you, thank you!"

"We really got lucky" replies Mace, as he continues, smiling graciously, "that canyon and the worn down roads came together perfectly. I figured you can't rebuild that bridge, but it already kind of needed to be redone." The three laugh for a moment, then begin walking back across the battle-hardened Bridge of Valeena.

Mace takes a deep victory breathe while overlooking the vast canyon beneath them, "Even with the solid planning, had just one of those hyracs stopped outside that gully we'd of been slaughtered."

Brutus pauses and looks out down the open trench when Mace says, "I already checked Brutus, it got em all."

"What now, do you think they'll send more?" asks Keila.

"Nah, I doubt it", replies Mace, "They reported to their commander yesterday that they had spotted a few UO soldiers here and today they lost him along with over a thousand troops. I think the Sirians will stay away from Valeena for now, it won't be worth it to them after this."

Brutus says, "I agree, and that means it's time for us to leave."

Keila thanks them again and apologetically tells Mace that she must stay and reorganize her people or she would see to their departure personally. He tells her that they understand and that he and Brutus can manage on their own.

Mace is happy for the Midians, but discouraged that he could not uncover more about the Sirian's intentions. Just before they leave, Collo runs past with the deceased Sirian Commander's helmet sitting crudely atop his head. The oversized headdress flops about and gives them all a laugh as Collo playfully stumbles around. As the jubilant little Midian moves on, Mace notices an odd symbol engraved into the back of the Sirian's armor, it was unlike any mark he had ever seen before, yet it somehow appeared familiar to him. He walks back over to the charred body of the Sirian Commander and as the cadaver gets closer, it hits him. He had seen those markings before, in pictures he had once viewed while researching the Nexcins. But the images he's thinking of were from battles centuries ago, so why would this Sirian be sporting one now? Mace ponders for a moment, then as he reaches the Commander's body he immediately begins to search it. The strange engraving can seen branded onto several areas of the highly decorated Commander, many times lined with an unfamiliar looking, bronze-like metal. Inside one of the scorched pouches, concealed behind one of the Sirian's bulky armorplates, Mace finds an infidisk. These are small chips, sometimes no larger than a pinhead that usually hold a limited amount of information or software. Mace wonders exactly what it's contents may withhold and secures the disk inside his own armor, he and Brutus then leave Valeena and begin the trek back to their ship.

They navigate the Midian tunnel system one last time and make it to the ship safely. Brutus is anxious to get back into space and away from the Sirians.

Once they board he asks Mace, "Continue to the Delinon System?"

Mace ignores Brutus as he is intent on trying to make sense of what he sees on this infidisk. All that comes up on the ship's computer is a listing of encrypted numbers. Mace runs the sequences through the UO database and results for the numbers' origins come back with a ninety-eight percent rate of accuracy on one grouping from the set. They are routing numbers from a commerce account of some sort. Now the tired soldier must rely on the UO's analysts to find out what bank and from what planet the routing number exists, along with whatever else this disk may hold.

Brutus again says, "Mace, continue on mission?"

Finally he replies, "No, go back to Galfin Bena. I think we have a new mission."

The two then take off and sneak away from the Sirian fleet undetected. Hopefully this infidisk will lead to a much needed break in Mace's universal crimelord theory and get them closer to identifying the parties behind it all. Perhaps the Sirians have been the missing link in connecting the universe-wide crime syndicate known as the Org to Narel or anyone else who is behind all the corruption and deception.

One Little Problem

It's now the year 2520, the two man team of Mace Crimson and Brutus Callous have been sent to a very private planet named Aclysia in order to further research the potential alliance between the Org, The Sirians and possibly Narel. After their run in with the Sirians on Valeena; Mace, Brutus, and certain others within the UO have spent the past few years tracking down pieces of scattered data evidence in search of a link between the three. Finally, they caught a break when a UO analyst put together a sequence of routing numbers that led them to this planet, formally titled Aclysia 3 as it is the third home world of the ancient Aclysian race. They are an extremely superior civilization which has been around the Verse for over ten million years, give or take a little. Solid records on the Aclysians are extremely rare due to their unusual need for privacy. They don't even allow the Universal Census to record their population readings; the Aclysians are just one of those races who prefer keeping to themselves, and to an extent that is their right. They are also widely considered to be one of the most unfriendly groups of people in Universe, as they are notorious for being unable to get along with beings that are of any race other than their own. Many attribute this personality flaw to their small physical stature and the liabilities to their psyche that this has caused over time. You see while exceedingly intelligent, a fully matured Aclysian male usually only reaches about three-and- a-half feet in height and eighty-five pounds in weight, based on average gravity. They are covered with fur all over their tiny bodies with the possibility of two diverse hair colors, white or dark green. This variation in fur shade is due to the two types of Aclysian that have evolved; one of which developed in the jungles of the southern hemisphere back on their original home world, the other lived in the mountainous regions of the Northern hemisphere.

Over the centuries their intelligence has proved to outweigh their physical shortcomings extensively. Some fairly recent advances have alone proven this feat; just a few centuries ago the Aclysian government developed a military battle suit that would soon revolutionize how they were perceived. It was designed to help Aclysian soldiers command their recently created police robots, termed RATS. This stood for Robotic Automated Tactical Support. These RATS were developed to patrol the streets of Aclysia so that citizens would not have to police one another, however since the RATS thought fairly independently they were deemed unfit to police the general population without supervision. This is where the battle suits came in. The Aclysian battle suit was designed as a six-legged, hydraulic controlled, armor and motion suit. The armor it displays is extremely dense and quite heavy, yet the advanced hydraulic systems still manage to allow for friction free movements. The suit gives it's Aclysian controller the ability to double their normal size and speeds up their movements by over three hundred percent. With this advancement the Aclysians had finally gained the physical strength needed to deal with the largest and strongest species in the Universe hand to hand. The six hydraulic legs make it highly maneuverable and the onboard computer's reaction speed as well as extremely fluid motions took melee combat to a whole new level for the race. The suit was incredibly adequate in every way and with these ingenious Aclysians operating them a physically weak species would quickly become one of the most feared around. The RATS used for policing were also tremendously effective in their task and crime in the cities of Aclysia dropped significantly. Soon the proud race would develop Army RATS; a superior model of battle robot which was designed for combat and would become known exclusively as RACS, which stood for Robotic Automated Conflict Support. The main difference between RACS and RATS is that the policing model floats on an electromagnetic cushion that exists between them and the metallic surface covering Aclysia. This helps when phasing and cannot be present on RACS due to the possibility that they'll need to leave the planet in a time of war. RACS instead walk on two legs and have a strong center of gravity which makes them a much more difficult enemy to fight. They typically walk upright, but the combat bots have four wheels built into their torso which they can drop down onto at any time for increased speed and mobility. Like

the Aclysian battle suits,RACS can sprout up to six arms. Only
two are present when originally deployed, however an additional
pair may spring from it's sides as well as a pair that may emerge from
the lower back. They are often equipped with various weapons
systems while also being trained and programmed to use a plasma
staff.

Less than a decade after the introduction of RACS, the entire
Aclysian army excluding officers consisted of the robotic soldiers
and almost every Aclysian citizen owned a battle suit of their own.
After a while the newly found toughness that the battle suits had
given its people proved hazardous. RATS could not easily police
Aclysians when wearing their battle suits as the Aclysian citizens
were now stronger than their robotic law enforcers and did not feel
any guilt over destroying RATS; they were simply machines.
Crime rates soared once again and it became clear that things
needed to change. The recreational use of battle suits was
outlawed, and from that point on a permit would be required to
operate one in public. The law was enacted swiftly and enforced
strictly, soon Aclysian Battle Suits were to be used on the surface of
Aclysia only for police and construction purposes. A model of
RATS that could phase was also created, which helped even out
the playing field against Aclysians who didn't want to give up their
battle suit without a fight. Phasing is the ability of beings or objects
to pass through solid material. Modern RATS can phase through
Aclysian made buildings and objects as if they were made
specifically for the task. They seamlessly manage to pass right
through most solid fixtures, physically altering their structure
slightly which allows them to vibrate through. This achievement
brought balance back to the planet because the Police RATS could
again easily control the streets.

As far as the mission goes, the UO Commanders Council has
decided that only a pair will be sent to Aclysia, this is the only way
to insure that they'll be given a fair chance to survey the situation.
The Council believes that any unit larger than two men will be
looked at by the Aclysians as a hostile infringement on their
privacy. Many soldiers working on this mission believe this to be a
political cop-out by the UO, fearing the ramifications of
aggravating the Aclysians at such an influential time is seen as a
weak move. For so long the UO had operated with minimal
political influence; their ironclad policy of only interfering in
universal matters kept them out of the contempt-filled views most

worlds and cultures have developed. Now, it seems as though Universal events have pulled the peacekeeping organization into a place they never wished to venture; political relations.

Lieutenant Lang recommended Mace and Brutus to his superiors for the mission, boasting that they were by far the best suited pair for the job. After hearing of their recent accomplishments, the Commanders wholeheartedly agreed. The tandem's orders on this mission were clear, but were not set in stone, it almost seemed as though the council was alluding that as long as their results deemed cause for their actions they'll be fine. While on Aclysia, Mace and Brutus are to first simply feel out their hosts, evaluating the Aclysians willingness to cooperate or lack thereof. After establishing this level of rapport they are to retrieve any plausible information that can be pulled from the Aclysian archives. Lieutenant Lang, who gave the team their final briefing, provided no further clarification on what's expected of them and was not at all specific to the boundaries of Mace and Brutus' authority. Upon leaving however, he tells them, "This may be our only chance, do whatever you have to and get that information".

This infidisk has put them one step closer, but they will need to find out exactly who's involved in order to uncover the true puppet masters behind recent events and attacks. Even more pressing of a question is why such diverse groups and individuals are cooperating with one another, as well as what their true objective may be.

Mace and Brutus both willfully accept the mission as they are beginning to realize how serious this situation with Narel has gotten. They both firmly believe that he has a plan to take over the Verse, a plan that has already been set in motion. Not much of this plan has been discovered as of yet, but the two know that Narel has a significant head start, so the roots of the unwinding plot must be exposed soon in order to stop or at least slow it down.

The only solid information Mace and Brutus have gathered about Narel's intentions are that his strategy involves the Org in an uncertain capacity, as well as the Sirians who are considered to be just an ally as they are too deeply embedded within the Centaur-Sirian war to jump into another mass conflict. The true end-game of Narel and his collaborators is still unknown. The goal of such an alliance must procure a hefty bounty in order to draw such a dramatically diverse group of conspirators and Mace believes that the only worthy expectation would be Universal conquest. Most of these theories are construed from hearsay and opinion, but even without any tangible evidence Mace is convinced that Narel has already laid the groundwork for the majority of this final attack; one in which he intends to destroy the UO entirely. In the eyes of his superiors and many others this is simply a glorified hunch, but Mace is more sure of it than any theory he's ever had. The question he seeks to answer now is simple, what's their enemy waiting for? If they can find something that's been left behind in the Org and Narel's tracks, or maybe something he is still seeking now, maybe they'll be able to identify what his next steps will be. Then, hopefully the plan can be pieced together and the core attack could be stopped before it begins.

All time-periods and activities of Narel since his apparent resurrection are still unknown, and despite numerous sightings around the Verse there has yet to be a confirmed identity verification anywhere. Several UO Commanders are beginning to entertain the idea that there is a conglomerate enemy out there, but after the failure on Galfin Bena it is still difficult for them to make a strong case with their peers. Few, if any believe that Narel is alive, and the current, commonly applied combination of The Org and the Sirians simply doesn't make sense to them. Unless the Commanders can be convinced that Narel has returned, there will be no way to gain enough support within the UO to properly combat this enemy. In more ways than one, this may be the last chance for Mace and company to unveil this threat.

The two UO soldiers arrive on Aclysia two days after receiving their orders. They have been thoroughly and perhaps unnecessarily briefed on the Aclysians as both Mace and Brutus have dealt with members of their race before. The team's basic plan is to show ample respect to the proud beings and try to make the Aclysians feel both esteemed and in control. If they achieve this, then maybe the ill-mannered little brats will stay out of their way, and perhaps even be helpful to the mission.

Their ship approaches the glowing planet, one which is teeming with bright lights from the countless cities below. From a high orbit they alert their hosts with an arrival code and are given permission to land once an escort ship arrives to guide them into the Prime Governor's Office Complex.

The Aclysians use a system of territories to control their capitol planet. Each territory has a Governor who presides over a designated geographical area, creating and adjusting laws in order to best suit the territory. The Prime Governor is the one being who outranks all other governors planet-wide and the only one who can veto their territorial laws. The Prime Governor Shuk Dah Lilaan is waiting to greet the UO ambassadors as he assuredly questions their intentions for visiting his planet. All the UO has told Aclysian Officials is that they're investigating a serious threat to Universal Security, one that may put all beings in jeopardy. The Aclysians cannot decline a request of that magnitude which is probably the only reason they agreed to grant this visit in the first place.

Mace and Brutus await their escort and talk briefly about how they'll approach the situation when their face to face with the Prime Governor.

Brutus says, "They already don't trust us. Maybe we should just come right out with it, if we tell him the truth the Governor may respect the honesty enough to help us out. I don't like all this deceit; it's not the way to treat a supposed ally."

Mace replies, "Well they could just as easily be our enemy. We need to divulge as little of what we know as possible, while accepting all the information we can; even if that means taking it."

Brutus sighs, "If that's your plan, then we may leave here with a new enemy after all and I don't think the lieutenant will be too happy about that."

"Yea" says Mace, "well if we tell them what we're looking for and they've already sided with Narel, we won't be leaving here at all. You and I have both dealt with Aclysians before, is it so hard to believe that they'd side with a tyrannical warlord who seeks to exploit and destroy the weaker races of the Verse? All while trading with and further enriching the wealthy and superior. Does that really sound far-fetched to you?"

Brutus quickly answers, "Aclysians aren't..."

He pauses and thinks for a second about what he was going to say, "Point taken, I'll shut up."

Their escort ship arrives, bursting up to within a few hundred feet of their fighter. Two large rods poke out from the sides of the Aclysian transport. The Rods extend up into the air and then make a ninety degree turn before continuing to extend out another few feet. A large energy beam then appears instantaneously, stretching between the two rods with a pulsating green glow. A bright light on the ship is then triggered and appears directly behind the beam. The beam now moves towards them slowly, coming to within inches of the ships armor. It then begins to move up and down the fighter adjusting to every nook and crevice with the light moving behind it simultaneously, always remaining in close synchronization. As it works over the entirety of the small vessel the UO ship begins to glow inside and out with a misty green radiance.

Mace looks down as the odd mist radiates off his armor and says, "I'm not sure if we should be worried, but this doesn't look good. Why is everything glowing?"

Brutus stares at the beam for a moment, he than says, "I know what that is."

He continues to stare at the beam.

Mace looks to Brutus, "Well do you wanna share buddy?"

Brutus comes out of his trance, "Yea, sorry it's a new type of surface scanner. It uses hundreds of different energy rays to create a near perfect model of it's target exposing any and all contraband. The beam can penetrate any solid in the known Verse, illuminating the true contents of its subject down to the particle level. It can detect explosives, weapons, stowaways; anything you would try to hide. You couldn't hide a chip the size of an electron aboard this ship without that thing finding it. I had heard the Julians were the first to develop one that didn't cause serious side effects on beings incidentally scanned by the beam, but even they were still in the experimental phases."

Mace replies, "Well I hope this one is past that stage."

"Me to", says Brutus as he points out the window at the large scanner, "The one I've read about only seemed to use one beam. This outer beam must have been developed to filter the energy concentration in some way, hopefully protecting us. The Aclysians are pioneers in detection systems, it's likely they've done their homework."

"Im glad we don't have anything to hide" says Mace sarcastically.

The Aclysians finish their scan and signal the ship to follow them in.

Mace follows right behind the agile Aclysian craft as they dip into the busy traffic of the bustling planet's skyways. Almost every Aclysian citizen flies a personal spacecraft and because of their high intelligence they are taught to do so at a very young age. Because of their size, the craft they fly are usually very small and easy to maneuver. This has its advantages and disadvantages for daily Aclysian traffic. It means that there's a lot more room on the skyway, but it also has provoked them to drive extremely fast and often times quite dangerously.

As Mace attempts to follow the medium sized Aclysian scanning ship, he begins to lose it in the sea of tiny Aclysian vessels weaving in and out of his airspace. Mace stays careful not to clip anyone, but he doesn't want to get lost either.

Brutus says, "You're gonna lose him and that's not gonna be good."

Mace replies, "I can't collide with a civilian either, that would be worse. I won't lose him, relax."

Mace sees a small gap and abruptly makes a move for the free space. As he does, the spot rapidly begins to close up, several Aclysians have broken course and rush towards the vacant opening. A few of the natives get there just before what on this planet can only be referred to as the bulky UO fighter, but even with the extra size and weight Mace refuses to be denied. While still approaching the now crowded traffic gap he makes a quick banking maneuver, then spins the fighter around one-hundred and eighty degrees.

He tells Brutus, "Fire off the two backup oxygen tanks."

Brutus locates the control levers to both backup tanks and pulls the release for the highly pressurized gas. It begins to frantically discharge from the tail of the fighter and Mace turns his thrusters around as though he wanted to fly in reverse. The gas from the oxygen tanks blows forcefully out the back of the UO ship while inertia from the thrusters continues to propel the ship backwards. Mace tries to hold it steady using his landing cameras to steer and aiming the gas leakage right into the wake of their escort ship. The force of the pressurized gas knocks dozens of civilian ships harmlessly out of the way, luckily enough their reckless driving habits have produced excellent safety features for personal spacecraft. Even if they do bump or collide, percussion bags and safety jets prevent serious injury.

The stunt proves successful as the UO team spins back around with a clear path ahead of them and is able to catch up with their escort just minutes before it reaches their destination. The two breathe a sigh of relief as they reach their hosts. The Governor's private docking platform appears to be where they'll land and the Prime Governor's complex which sits before them is quite an incredible image. It spans nearly a thousand stories high and over ten miles in length, the soldiers cannot even see an end to the building when looking to the east, and only the faintest edge can be seen off in the distance to the west. Quite the spectacle by the standards of any race. It is the Prime Governor's main center of operations and the largest stronghold on the planet. There are over a million RACS patrolling the fortified complex, not to mention around ninety thousand battle suited Aclysian officers.

Mace and Brutus can see the exponential army presence as they make their approach and when they turn their attention to the streets outside of the fortress it doesn't look much better. There, the police RATS seem so take over for the military and can be seen populating the streets with more density than the Aclysian citizens.

Mace finishes his approach and lands successfully on the designated spaceport adjacent to their guide ship. The corroded complex has several spaceports on its rooftops, yet the massive fortress somehow maintains a medieval-type look. This ramshackle appearance was due to the Aclysians unusual work ethic. Oddly enough, they labor without rest on ideas or inventions while in production or development, perfecting every detail and improving every engineering aspect that they can in order to never have the need for upkeep or maintenance on anything they own. In turn, they do not upgrade or improve finished projects or items unless the advancement is rather significant, looks and superficial values are meaningless to their people so restoration has become nearly obsolete. As long as a product remains constantly efficient, it remains acceptable. Their rule of thumb for centuries has been if it needs routine maintenance or repair within a normal lifetime, then it's simply not good enough. They see general upkeep as a waste of time, believing that if it had just been made right the first time it would never need to be repaired at all. A strange philosophy, but it has created a way of life that works extremely well for them, demonstrated vividly by the race's success.

Although the Governor's Complex has the general appearance of a typical building, at least the outer layer of the structure seems to be composed of a dense alloy shell of some sort. The worn down, semi-eroded metal gives the massive fortress a weakened image, a misconception easily cleared up once the architects are remembered. If the Aclysian's reputation holds true, this building is probably as structurally sound and impenetrable as the day it was built.

After landing, Mace and Brutus exit their ship. The duo is swiftly approached by several Aclysians wearing their fabled battle suits. Mace is always surprised at how agile these suits make the frail and arrogant beings, just by the fluidness of their strides and limb motions one can tell that the suit is quite an engineering marvel. Each movement of the six legs, whether individually or in unison appears fluent and flawless, unlike some other models of hydraulic combat suits the UO soldiers have encountered around the Verse. The armor appears to be made of an alloy which neither soldier is familiar with and the part of the suit which surrounds the Aclysian himself leaves little flesh unshielded. Due to this, it's no surprise that Mace and Brutus are not even asked to relinquish their plasma staffs.

One of the Aclysians says, "Follow us humans, the Prime Governor awaits word of your arrival."

So Mace and Brutus follow the three Aclysian officers into the complex. The interior structure is oddly designed, extremely wide corridors lead directly into long and narrow ones. Some of the halls were lined with doorways, yet some contained none at all. Nothing was painted or primed, just faded alloys or carbonboard stretching across all the floors, walls, and ceilings. There were also winding staircases and bi-levels with doors in the most random of locations; on corners or amidst a break in stairwells, often seeming misplaced. They are brought to a large elevator that will carry them deep down into the palace. The doors close and they begin to descend, dropping over two thousand stories rapidly and sending them into the sub-levels of the enormous fortress.

Mace and Brutus share the elevator with the three Aclysians, so not much is said. The two do share an uneasy look as they both ponder why the elevator seems to be descending so far into the complex. Finally, they reach the end of the line, sub-level two hundred. The two exit the elevator and follow their escorts down another long, narrow hallway. As Brutus and Mace rode the elevator they briefly saw the lavish designs and décor of the deep inner palace which in contrast to everything else they've seen, looked most beautiful. Once they reach sub-level two hundred however, it is far from beauty. They emerge from the elevator into a hallway which looks very old, dilapidated, and is dimly lit. The walls are crumbling and cracked with a matching stone floor that appears to be ancient and eroded. Finally they come to the end of the hall which leads to a single door. The door is opened and yet another shocking backdrop appears before them. They peer into a room filled with food, games, entertainment monitors, and all types of Aclysian recreational items. This is meant to be seen by the two as a courteous gesture, but Mace and Brutus are not so easily fooled.

The Aclysian soldier walks inside and tells them, "This is the Prime Governor's waiting area. You will remain here during your stay whenever you are not with the Governor."

Mace jumps at this statement, "Exactly when is it that we'll be seeing him? The reason for our visit is not recreation."

The Aclysian replies with false regret, "I understand, but you must recognize that our Prime Governor is quite busy and the fact that he's allowed this meeting to take place at all is an acknowledgement of his concern. You'll wait here for as long as it takes and if you're lucky his schedule will free up enough for the governor to summon you and discuss whether or not he can help the UO. Now back away from the door."

Mace and Brutus back up and the Aclysians close the door, locking them into the so called waiting room. Mace tries to override the door controls, but it's no use the exit is sealed shut.

Brutus asks, "So what do you think this is?"

"I'm not sure", Mace answers, "I guess right now we just have to wait it out. They only gave us twenty four hours of clearance, how long can they make us wait?"

Brutus laughs and says, "You don't think that food is poisoned, do you?"

Mace replies, "I sincerely doubt it, if they wanted to kill us in this place they wouldn't need to use poison."

"Good, cause I'm starving" Brutus replies..

The hungry soldier eats like he hadn't done so in years and Mace follows suit picking out a much more balanced meal. After they're done they try to pass the time by talking and watching Universal Television on one of the entertainment monitors. Information on the recent increase in attacks around the Verse, as well as some harsh criticism of the UO crowds the news stations. Brutus argues with the screen for a few minutes until he becomes frustrated and changes the channel to a Tringalean sporting event known as Gollo Ball. Despite the stalling, the UO needs to take advantage of this opportunity. So for now, the two will remain patient as they wait for their host.

The hours continue to pass however and the two soldiers eventually begin to feel like they're not even going to see the Prime Governor at all. After nearly six hours of waiting Brutus really starts to get anxious, Mace stands beside the door where he's had his ear pressed tightly against metal for nearly forty-five minutes.

Brutus says, "Why even bring us here if he's not going to see us?"

Mace replies, "For appearances I would guess, to make it appear to outsiders as though they tried to help."

Brutus lets out an aggravated sigh, "What are you even listening for?"

Mace walks away from the door and over to the bathroom where he begins to inspect the ceiling.

He tells Brutus, "There's at least two, probably three of those Aclysian soldiers still outside the door."

Brutus replies, "Not to mention the other million or so military personnel that occupy this fortress."

Mace responds, "Very true, but even three is more than I wanna deal with. Whe…"

Suddenly the monitor they had been watching U.T.V. on loses sound and goes blank. They look to the screen where an Aclysian wearing a lavish golden robe and a modified battle suit can be seen.

It is the Prime Governor and he is using the monitor as a video link. He says to the two soldiers, "Greetings my UO friends. I apologize for being held up, I hope you have found your accommodations suitable while I was delayed."

The two soldiers both walk over and stand directly in front of the screen.

Mace replies, "Yes Prime Governor, they've been quite suitable, but we were hoping to work with you on solving a Universal problem, not sit in a dungeon for nearly six hours."

"I do sincerely apologize for the wait, but you understand that problems on my planet must always come first", responds the Governor as his tone gradually becomes more condescending, "Even if that means being put before these claimed Universal Issues. Now tell me, what exactly is this matter of such grave importance?"

Mace explains to the Governor, "We need to trace a trail of funds, equipment, and treasonous information that may have left remnants in your planet's information bank. From what we've uncovered already our analysts believe that most of the data we need can still be retrieved from your archives. This small favor could provide us with a huge boost to our investigation, which I assure you Governor is indeed of Universal importance. So, when can we expect you to come get us? As soon as we check your system we'll be on our way."

The Governor appears to half attempt holding back a smirk and tells him, "Well unfortunately there's gonna be a problem with that. As you know I'm a very busy leader, and matters dealing with my people tend to be much more complex than a human could understand. I will not be able to meet with you in person, nor will I allow you access to our archives, that's a security threat to my people you see. I do however want to assure you that your job has been done today Sergeant Crimson; you've made us aware of what to look for and we will be sure to scan our databases for any plausible leads. Any conspicuous data found by my people will be immediately turned over to the UO. Thank you for bringing this matter to our attention and I'm sure the Order will keep you updated on our progress. You'll have to remain on the planet for another three hours, that's the earliest time I could get you a departure escort so feel free to enjoy the recreations of the waiting room until your shuttle arrives. Thank you again for your patience soldiers and for your devotion to keeping the Universe safe, for all of us."

The Governor then signs off of the video link.

Brutus shouts at the now blank screen, "That's it, you could of at least lied better than that! We should have reasoned with him, even told him about Narel. That woulda gotten these arrogant scrap piles' attention."

Mace begins to walk back over to the bathroom and continues to inspect the ceiling just as he had before the Governor intervened. He tells Brutus, "It doesn't matter what we do or say, he never intended to help us. The esteemed governor wanted to use us for the same reason we wanted to use him, information."

Brutus hops in and mutters, "At least we're somewhat honest about it".

Mace continues, "The question now seems to be, is he just a smug Aclysian who thinks the smallest of his eight fingers is smarter than both of us? Or is he actually part of this and covering the tracks of his allies. We can't leave here until we find out."

Brutus thinks aloud, "Well we're locked in the basement of an impenetrable military citadel belonging to one of the most highly aggressive and highly advanced races known. How exactly do you intend to find out anything?"

"Well this room is pretty solid, no windows or access points. We can't get out the front entrance, so I think I'm going to have to take the architect's exit."

Mace opens his plasma staff and cuts off a metal vent protruding from the wall uncovering a large, elongated air duct than runs up into the palace. He climbs into the duct as Brutus says, "Of course let's go climbing through the fanatical Aclysian's air ducts, why didn't I think of that?"

Once inside Mace tells Brutus, "I'm gonna go see if I can find an active computer terminal and hack into their system. I brought an infidisk, so I can copy anything I find."

"Well I'm going with you", Brutus proclaims, "if they find out your gone I don't wanna be here to bear the consequences."

"You have to stay here", Mace quickly responds, "I'll be back before the three hours are up, but someone needs to be here in case they open the video link back up to check on us."

"So what am I supposed to say if they ask where you are?" Says Brutus.

Mace climbs further into the duct and tries to close the vent off behind him the best that he can, "Just say I'm in the bathroom or something."

Mace then disappears into the dark vent shaft, leaving behind Brutus who anxiously returns to the waiting room.

Back on Utopera, within the UO's primary base of operations, Major Parra and Lieutenant Lang argue with two of their Commanders; Gala Ziel and Freen Yareh. Gala Ziel is a female Sirian and Freen Yareh is a Male Tringalean. They've both been commanders in the UO for a very long time, serving that time and their cause with distinction and honor. Both are recognized as great warriors, but Commander Yareh is commonly acknowledged as one of the strongest soldiers in the Universe.

The four have been talking about the possible link between the Org and Narel. This is not the first time that the Major has tried to discuss this, but the Commanders as a whole remain reluctant to take the possibility seriously, let alone listen to arguments on the issue. In most cases this is likely out of either fear or doubt, whichever reason would be inexcusable.

Major Parra says, "We've been able to link the Org and the Sirians with one another indirectly, through numerous back-channel funds, co-investor projects, and other allocations. Most however are networked through an unknown third party, one who seems to be the coordinator of the entire operation. We also have uncovered figures that lead us to believe the alliance has predetermined the payoff that each party would acquire should they be successful in destroying the UO. Here too we see a pattern that appears to distribute properties across the Verse to three parties, likely the main conspirators behind this plot."

Major Parra switches on a computer generated graph that maps the Universe called a Unichart. The graph is a pop-out, holographic, three-dimensional touch display that allows access to all the different zones of the Verse simply by reaching out and grabbing that particular section of space. Areas can be pulled and pushed aside, or drug in any direction to bring up the necessary segment of the Universe. When a zone is pulled up and enlarged it expands into a full breakdown of all the systems within it which can also be expanded as needed. The Major flips through all the habitable systems of the Verse with about one-fifth of them depicted in red and another one-fifth highlighted in gold. These were assumed to be the star systems that the Org and the Sirians would claim. The rest of the Verse was left blank; sixty percent of the galaxies, solar systems, colonies, and asteroids, all left unclaimed. This leads them to believe that Narel would control this portion of the Verse with absolute authority.

Commander Ziel who now almost seems to be offended by the Major's claims ignores the map and berates him, "So you're insinuating that they are planning an active assault on the

Universal Order; The Org, The Sirian Race, and a third unknown participant? Do I have to remind you that we are not only respected in this Universe, but we are feared Major. No one without a sheer suicide on their mind is planning an attack on us."

Commander Yareh adds, "Let's cut the politics Major, this isn't an active council session; the third party you're referring to is Narel. The question is, why should we believe you? Assuming he has somehow returned, he's not shown any real aggression towards us, which certainly contrasts his past approach. According to you he's been around for longer than we know, so why would he suddenly attempt a mass attack? Would it not be wiser to cause a politically anchored Universal War against a protector of the state such as ourselves? This would cause us to spread forces out thin and get bogged down into a long, drawn out conflict. A tactic warlord's often seem to use to their advantage."

Lieutenant Lang answers to the surprise of Major Parra as well as both superiors, "Well, Commander, we think that may be the essence of his attack. By diverting from what would seem to be the expected approach of a tyrant, he adds yet another element of deception to his scheme. At this point we believe he's been waiting and planning for many years, perhaps staying patient until just the right sequence of events creates just the right situation; remaining invisible to the masses and only lingering within the minds and cultures of the Verse as a ghost story. He uses his seeming non-existence and the story of his death to cause doubt and confusion within the minds of all those who have contributed to stopping him in the past, the UO being number one on this list. The brightest minds of the UO and most other places say that he's been long dead, so any sane person naturally would believe the same thing. This has only further clouded the perception of the warlord and makes all who proclaim his actual physical existence appear to be nothing more than lunatics or conspiracy theorists. Were this to in fact be the case, and Narel has anticipated our actions leading up to this very moment, he could have only hoped for officers such as Commander Ziel to simply sweep these occurrences under the rug without so much as an unbiased evaluation."

Commander Ziel stands up angrily and shouts, "You're severely out of line Lieutenant!"

Lang realizes that he has overstepped his bounds, "I apologize commander, that was uncalled for."

"Yes it was" says Ziel, "I'm tempted to end this session and make your insubordination a matter of record."

Commander Yareh now jumps in, "That won't be necessary Commander Ziel, everyone seems to have passion when it comes to this topic let's just keep the discussion informal. Now continue Lieutenant."

Commander Ziel is not happy, but she sits back down without a word and the Lieutenant continues.

"An all or nothing attack under the correct circumstances and at absolutely the most opportune time has been shown throughout history to be the most effective way of insuring victory. He's been in and out of the EV database for centuries now, never exhibiting a clear motive for any of his actions even before his most recent death. It has always been assumed that he was just an anomaly, one that would be too difficult to destroy hence better left alone. That's up until Hashin finally destroyed him and ended his reign of terror. Before he died, the UO and he were at an unsolvable stalemate, he could not destroy the UO and the UO seemingly could not get rid of him. Then, Commander Hashin, the only soldier that any betting soul would ever think had a chance against him; gets an incredible break and corners the warlord after a severely uncharacteristic mistake. Hashin fights just as well if not better than any reasonable person could predict, defeating Narel in an epic showdown. The unspoken-about black cloud of the Universe was gone once again, but what if it was all done by design? One small step after another, possibly even allowing his own death to further the ultimate goal, putting an end to the UO once and for all."

Commander Ziel aggressively steps back in, "But like you said, he was destroyed by Tagithus as we all know, cut into pieces and burned to ash in front of hundreds of spectators. Narel's lunacy is common knowledge, even if he was insane enough to think that death would further his goal, such a thought would not resurrect him. No race or being can bring one back from the grave, so why are you wasting our time talking about ghosts and creating unnecessary speculation that could be perceived as borderline treason. This conversation is…"

Commander Yareh intervenes once again, "We all know what this conversation is Commander, but we all came here today knowing we were going to have it. The current Versal situation definitely appears as though some type of intricate plot could possibly be under way and we are all under obligation to entertain such possibilities. Now if you want to leave Commander, please feel free to excuse yourself, but know that this conversation is going to finish with or without you. Now, please continue Lieutenant."

Commander Ziel gives in, choosing to stay and listen.

"I'll get to the point Commanders, the time lapses between his actions and subtle covert missions have made his true objective a complete mystery. I, along with several other team members have studied this man and the scenario that's unfolded with open minds and unbroken concentration; we've backtracked the slightest instances and examined every angle. Truthfully speaking, I wouldn't be sure that even his own allies know the true depth of his plan. Only he knows the actual plot and exact time at which to unleash it."

Commander Ziel steps in once again, adding, "Please, tell us more about your unsanctioned team. The one making little progress if any while the rest of our soldiers scamper around the Verse with one of the highest workloads we've ever witnessed".

Lieutenant Lang continues quickly, his voice deepening as he blatantly hides his frustration, "Once everything he believes necessary is in place he will assault us, and I assure you Commanders, that time is coming. We've delayed this attack with our soldiers in the field, who throughout the past few years have slowed both Narel's attempts to gain power and the Org's immense expansion. Two of my boys single-handedly stopped him from obtaining Lapiils that could have brought a sure end to Utopera. If the impending attack is ever launched it will be the pinnacle of preparation, a chance that he has waited for more than a lifetime to attain. If he went for the Lapiils he must be close. This enemy has studied us, he's worked long and hard to devise a plan that will not be halted by even time itself so that when he does strike, there will be no defense capable of stopping him. Read any of the notorious war quotes from the UO archives, the words of history's greatest Commanders clearly explain that if this is in fact Narel's plan, it's going to work."

The Lieutenant pulls out a book entitled Words of War, and begins pointing out excerpts quoted from some of the most notable warriors throughout the ages. He begins to read off quotes quickly yet articulately in a desperate attempt to make his point.

"Be extremely subtle, even to the point of formlessness. Be extremely mysterious, even to the point of soundlessness. Thereby, you can be the director of your opponent's fate."

"He who is prudent and lies in wait for the enemy who is not, will be victorious"

"If you know the enemy and know yourself, you need not fear the results of a hundred battles"

Commander Ziel gasps and drops back into her chair unimpressed while Commander Yareh continues to seem engrossed. The sight of the Commander's interest fuels Lang to continue.

"The victorious strategist only seeks battle after the victory has been won, whereas he who is destined for defeat fights first and afterward seeks victory."

"What is of supreme importance in war, is to attack the enemies strategy"

"Pretend inferiority and encourage enemy arrogance"

"It's right here in the words of our greatest minds, "proclaims Lang, "some coming from Tagithus himself. Every one of these can be applied to our situation and imply our ignorance as well as Narel's apparent foresight."

Commander Ziel can contain herself no longer and yells out harshly, "I've heard enough."

"One more!" exclaims Lang as he flips to the final page of the book, "If you are ignorant of both your enemy and yourself, you are certain to be in peril."

The Commander is now outraged once again, "Who do you think you're speaking to Lieutenant? If you're looking for some acknowledgment or praise for your homework then you're in the wrong business."

The Lieutenant tries to speak, "I'm n…

At this point the Commander simply won't hear it, "What proof do you have of all this? In the Universal Order quotes from great warriors do not constitute as actual evidence. You claim that you don't want to be perceived as a conspiracy theorist, but if you've been pushing your theory with no real evidence it makes you just that. Narel is not lying in wait, he is lying in pieces until proven otherwise. So where is the proof?"

Lieutenant Lang replies, "Well we still don't have any solid proof besides the infidisk, but I currently have a team following a critical lead recovered from that disk. They're on Aclysia as we speak. When they return hopefully we'll have something more."

Commander Ziel's voice escalates, "So these astronomical accusations and insubordinate lectures are backed up without any plausible evidence? Just an infidisk that MAY possibly lead to something substantial."

She pauses and gives an eery smirk before continuing with an even more sarcastic tone, looking over the Lieutenant and then onto the Major. "Oh, now I'm a believer…I didn't know that you MAY have something more stable in the works. I'd expect this from a human, but you Major Parra? The team you've sent to Aclysia consists of two humans as well, correct?"

Commander Yareh finally cuts in, "That is irrelevant and you know it Commander."

Ziel nods apologetically to her fellow Commander then continues to berate, "We don't need unrest inside our Order, especially with how thin we're already spread throughout the Verse. Narel is a powerful being, we know this, but even if he were to be alive he is still simply a petty warlord with no backing from any known peoples. We have nothing to fear from him and if by some chance he is around; one day when he's old and weak he'll again serve justice for the crimes he's perpetrated. If he truly has sat around and hid for all this time, need we really even fear him any longer?"

"Narel always was a risk", responds the Major, "even if you haven't took notice. One far too big for us to overlook any longer. He's not just another warlord, he's something different. If we don't destroy this threat, it will destroy us."

As Ziel prepares to dig into the Major, Commander Yareh ends the conversation without further debate, "We shall see my friends. Let's hope your boys bring back something we can make sense of. Now we have a recruit gauntlet session which should have started ten minutes ago, thank you for the briefing officers. You're assessment has been well received."

Both Commanders excuse themselves while Lang and Parra remain seated, visibly frustrated by how the meeting transpired.

The Lieutenant lets out a frustrated gasp, "It seems like the only way the Council will truly accept this threat is if a Nexcin Fleet shows up on Utopera's doorstep."

"Let's hope not" says Major Parra, "If he's managed to stay hidden this long Narel won't come out from under his rock until we've already lost."

"Ziel certainly flip-flopped enough in her logic", says the Lieutenant as he begrudgingly gathers his things. "First Narel adamantly doesn't exist, then she suddenly has faith that one day he'll serve justice for his crimes? You make any sense of that?"

Parra replies, "She clearly has an agenda, but with her it could be anything. For all we know she could be involved, after all she is a Sirian. We'll have to worry about it later, I have an operations meeting that I need to prep for."

While the higher ups on Utopera continue to struggle with the idea that Narel is up to something, Sergeant Crimson remains in pursuit of the evidence that can make up their minds. Once he begins scaling the long vent shaft, Mace quickly realizes that all the access points have been sealed. He speculates that this predicament is probably only present within the complex Sub-levels, so if he can get to the surface levels of the facility he'll be able to find an accessible exit. The one good thing about the Aclysians being so small is that the levels of their complex aren't very far apart and Mace can climb from floor to floor without exerting too much energy. As he moves up swiftly and steadily, RATS can be felt as they phase and pass through the empty shaft. The phasing process is silent, but Mace can feel the slight breeze left in their wake as they brush by him. The machines must use this large channel to patrol and move through the complex without disturbing the Aclysian personnel. As he proceeds, a few of the RATS graze him gently and give the soldier a slight scare; but as they don't believe anything is present within the shaft, the ignorant machines don't even notice. The darkness helps protect him from detection, but it also blinds the soldier to their incoming flight paths. He proceeds with great care in order not to make anymore noticeable contact with the reckless bots as they scurry about.

Despite this persistent obstacle, Mace climbs the two hundred sub-levels in less than an hour when he's abruptly stopped by a dead end. The vent shaft for the sub-levels must be kept separate from that of the main complex and despite his efforts he appears to be entirely sealed out.

Stumped for a moment, Mace uncharacteristically begins to become frustrated. The pressure he's been feeling lately is so immense, he needs to uncover a lead and this could be his last shot.

The seasoned soldier quickly calms himself and tries to explore the obstruction a bit, opening his plasma staff for light. He probes the exterior of the shaft with no result, that's until he crawls into the deepest corner of shaft wall. Here, he finds a small, narrow maintenance duct that was probably built for Aclysian technicians. He cuts the door open with his staff, catching the broken lock before it can drop the two hundred or so stories. The maintenance shaft does not continue upward into the palace, but as it is his only option Mace decides to proceed anyway. He manages to crawl and slide his way through the narrow tunnel and luckily ends up in the main elevator shaft, likely the same one which had taken him and Brutus down to the sub-levels when they arrived. This shaft runs through the extent of the complex and Mace can access any level he wishes from here. He begins climbing once again and checks each of the lower levels for the one that will be best suited for his objective.

On the seventh floor he locates an office that is not in use. This is the only level he's checked that doesn't have two or more RACS patrolling the elevator lobby. Mace now locates and climbs through the air ducts of the seventh level in order to get a better view of the office. He maneuvers and works his way through the tight confines of the Aclysian ductwork until he spots a mainframe connected to the central network. The cramped soldier can see that there are two RACS inside, standing guard just behind the terminal he so desperately needs. Mace is running out of time and realizes that he'll need to destroy these two if wants to get to that computer. He carefully positions himself overtop of the pair, careful not to make any noise that could bring them out of their dormant state as both RACS sit motionless on opposite sides of the room. The veteran warrior needs to be quick, as soon as they detect his presence he'll be identified as hostile. He then sizes up the shaft and opens his plasma staff, the duct itself is far too small for the weapon when fully extended so both plasma chambers puncture the duct's thin metal. He then twists the weapon while spinning around, cutting himself free with a single, solid stroke. Mace falls directly between the two RACS who rapidly turn to him after their sensors pick up the disturbance from his fall. One of them immediately fires a liquid plasma burst at him, spurting a thin green stream of plasma from the center of its chest. Mace quickly dodges the attack and the stream engulfs the second RAC in burning liquid plasma. The plasma throws it's sensors into a chaotic disarray and the machine bounces off several walls before falling over as its inner components are scorched and melted. Mace is now left with just one of these machine adversaries and it's standing right between him and the terminal. Mace fakes an attack and the robot shoots his plasma in slightly the wrong direction. Before the RAC can readjust, Mace wisely jumps him from the opposite side and stabs his staff right into the barrel of its main gun. This strategy proves efficient and with his plasma chamber punctured, the combat bot leaks the weaponized plasma all over itself, destroying its own circuitry. At last Mace receives his hard-earned chance to evaluate the Aclysian's files.

Down on sub-level two-hundred Brutus anxiously awaits the return of his friend. He's been rocking back and forth in his chair for some time now, impatiently looking over at the vent where Mace exited. Suddenly, and unexpectedly the Prime Governor reappears on the monitor.

Shocked and startled Brutus almost loses his balance before saying, "Governor, How are you?"

He responds, "Fine, I just wanted to check on you boys and let you know it looks like we might be able to get you outta here earlier than expected."

"Good", Brutus nervously replies, "That's just uh great Governor. Thank you."

The Governor looks around the room, at least what he can see through the monitor, "Where's your partner I wanted to wish him off as well?"

Brutus looks to the air vent and answers, "I don't know what you guys put in that buffet you left for us, but he's been in that bathroom since the last time we spoke with you."

The Governor laughs and replies, "I shouldn't have expected a human's stomach to be able to handle our cuisine. Well have a safe trip home private and good luck fixing that Universal problem of yours, we're all behind you."

Brutus responds, "I appreciate that Governor and thank you for all the hospitality."

The Governor closes the video link and Brutus takes a deep sigh of relief. He says to himself, "Yea great hospitality, I can remember battlefields where I felt more at ease....where are you Mace?"

As for his partner, Mace still hasn't made much progess in the abandoned office on level 7. He's having some trouble cracking the Aclysian's system, but eventually he breaks through, hacking the password of an Aclysian who works within this office. The soldier works through the files hastily, searching the Aclysian government's holdings and account records scanning for a match to the routing numbers they obtained on Valeena. After a few minutes of a total system scan however, the results come up empty.

Mace thinks and thinks, then he runs a more general search of the system, broadening it to include any arrangement of the routing number, along with any matches to other sequences from the infidisk. This time just a brief search yields several results for the numbers, yet there is something odd about the way in which the information is stored. It was embedded as if someone were meant to access it from outside the network, someone with extensive programming knowledge who would need to know the numbers as well as multiple passwords, procedures, and firewall sequences. No Aclysian within the network would ever attempt to access it, so Narel and his collaborators embed their own data within the system and let the Aclysians unknowingly guard it for them. The members of this evil alliance then pass through their own security parameters from outside the system and access the information through a back door of sorts. A tricky and clever way to hide knowledge right under the noses of so many unsuspecting bystanders, that is unless someone who's interested enough happens to stumble upon some of the data. Mace looks over the files and sees more evidence than he had ever imagined. Outlined in front of him is a hidden correspondence between the Org and Narel, along with several large accounts delegating funds allocated to locations all over the Verse. There was also a detailed breakdown of the UO populous including reserves, not to mention what appears to be intended UO targets. Mace will need to further assess the data back on Utopera to decipher all of the information that's been stored inside this network, so he begins to copy all the files relating to Narel's secret routing numbers onto his infidisk.

As they copy he continues to browse through the immensity of information. The soldier is amazed at what he's seeing. He'd hoped to find some small shred of evidence, just one solid link, but never something like this. Mace overlooks a detailed schematic of

Utopera with potential weak points in base defenses listed and analyzed to great detail. He also reads over several continuation plans, all apparently created for immediate implementation after the UO has been eliminated. One recurring ideal addresses any planet or system that resists the new regime, proclaiming that they will be destroyed in less than one day; it also says over and over again that no being nor group of beings shall ever be permitted to stand against Narel. Mace had finally found the evidence he was looking for, and it was nearly indisputable.

It seems as though Narel and/or the Org have buried these codes within the Aclysian mainframe and have probably exploited many other Systems and large scale networks as well. They've most likely embedded codes and hidden funds all over in a discrete and vague pattern to keep anyone from linking together the data, thus better avoiding detection. The information is encrypted in such a way that it is accessible from all over the Universe to those whose know how to unlock it. Unless you have the exact code sequence for unlocking the decryption it would be impossible to uncover, not to mention the fact that the best place to hide something is often the last place those interested would think to look. It's pretty ingenious when you think about it, the Aclysians have no cause nor reason to ever scan there systems for anything concerning Narel and the UO would normally have no reason to search the Aclysian files at all. Finding that infidisk on Kutchatar may prove to be the luckiest break that they could've hoped for. Without it the UO never would have known this complex system of subterfuge even existed. Narel probably chose star systems that were not allied to him purposely because they would never be linked or investigated in association with himself or his acts.

As Mace's download is nearing completion, he hears the elevator make a series of beeping noises. He runs out of the office and into the lobby where it can be seen that the elevator is on it's way down and is indeed stopping at the seventh floor. He rushes back into the office and grabs his disk just as it finishes. He closes down the monitor and quickly jumps back into the air duct, bending it back together the best that he can. Mace sits motionless inside the vent shaft as the clanks and clatter of metal on metal can be heard from the moment the elevator stops. It was a much louder noise than any of the RACS he's observed ever made. Suddenly, two RACS followed by a suited up Aclysian Commander march into the office. This must have been the cause of the extra noise, Mace wasn't expecting such a high-ranking officer to be out patrolling the fortress. The Aclysian looks around the room and for a moment focuses directly onto the vent shaft where Mace lies frozen in place, staring right back at him.

The air vent conceals him from the Aclysian, but the Commander barks at the RACS, "Check that computer for activity, someone was in here!"

Mace hears this and quietly starts squirming back toward the elevator shaft. The RACS he destroyed lye just a thin wall away from where the Commander stands. Mace makes his way back to the shaft quickly and climbs on top of the elevator. Using his plasma staff, he breaks into the untended elevator by cutting a hole through the ceiling while the Aclysian and his RACS are still busy checking the computer. Once inside he closes the elevator doors and heads straight back to sub-level 200. Now that he's got what they came for Mace needs to get his partner and escape with this evidence before the Aclysians inevitably figure out what's happened.

The elevator heads down the shaft and gets to sub-level 182 when it begins to violently shake. The Aclysian Commander must have discovered Mace's activity or found the remains of the desecrated RACS and they're already overriding the system. Mace instinctively jumps out of the elevator car through the same hole he broke in through and grabs on to some piping which runs up the side of the shaft. Moments later the elevator is abruptly lunged back up towards the waiting Aclysians, barely missing Mace who clings to the sturdy rows of pipe. Once it passes he begins climbing down the final eighteen stories, jumping from one to the next with relative ease. As is usually the case the trip down is much easier than the trip up and he reaches the bottom in no time.

The now rushed soldier soon gets to the two hundredth sub-level and has no time to waste with that Commander right on his tail. Instead of sneaking in, Mace begins to bang violently on the outside doors of the shaft. After about a minute, a RAT comes to the door and attempts to phase through it. Mace blocks his every try, pushing the stubborn machine back through his self-made entrance time and again. A RAC, also standing on the other side of the door becomes frustrated and pries them open with it's long metal arms. Mace is cleverly waiting for him in the shaft and as the combat bot peers out he slices deeply into the RAC with his plasma staff and pulls him into the shaft. He stabs once more, this time into the central processing unit of the bot, destroying it. Mace now jumps down into the open doorway and the RAT is floating right there. The crafty android erratically moves from side to side and begins aggressively firing single shot plasma rounds at Mace. Most of them miss, but he is forced to block a couple with his staff. As soon as the RAT overshoots him, Mace gives a big swing that slices a stabilizer clear off its left side. The RAT spins out of control and as it begins to spew out plasma Mace gives it a swift kick to guide the disoriented machine into the elevator shaft where it crashes violently into the wall and plummets to the ground. That takes care of them, now there's only one more RAC standing between him and his friend. This one just happens to be standing guard directly in front of Brutus' cell and has now moved into a fighting stance. The well-trained machine begins to advance. Mace knows that if he allows the RAC to get a shot on him at this range it will almost surely be lethal. The intuitive soldier pretends to be injured and retreats back into the elevator shaft. The RAC continues to advance cautiously, keeping it's battle stance as it proceeds. Once the RAC gets within about fifty feet of him, Mace jumps into the doorway and throws his plasma staff straight through it's head, terminating it instantly. The RAC's head explodes into a small burst before he can even react. The staff becomes lodged into its metal casing, knocking the inert hunk of metal to the ground. Mace grabs the staff and pulls it out of the RAC as he hurries past it on his way to the holding room. He unlocks the door and Brutus ignites his staff, preparing for an ambush.

"Expecting someone?" Mace says cockily.

Brutus breathes a sigh of relief and asks, "So how bad is it?"

Mace responds, "Let's just say we have to get outta here and now. I'm not exactly sure what's going on or who all is involved, but I got our evidence. Now we just have to get back to Utopera alive so we can use it."

Brutus runs in front of him back towards the door and Mace says, "No, they took the elevator. We need to use the vent; it leads all the way back up to the main elevator shaft. From there we can get out of this place and call for rescue."

As the two make their way to the bathroom they can hear the Prime Governor appear on their T.V. yet again.

"What do you think you're doing? How dare you betray our trust like this! You'll never escape! Answer me cowards!"

As he commands them to answer him, Brutus stops and takes out his plasma staff. He walks over to the monitor.

"Brutus come on", shouts Mace.

The Aclysian stares him in the eye through the video screen, "There you go, shed your human delusions. Be realistic and give yourself up."

Brutus replies, "How bout I show you some of your Aclysian hospitality", he then stabs his plasma staff through the screen.

He looks back to Mace, "Sorry to waste the time, but I'm really sick of that guy's voice."

Mace smiles before running back through the small bathroom and up into the vent once again. Brutus follows this time and they begin their climb for freedom.

As they ascend the shortened levels of the compact Aclysian facility, Brutus is relieved by the ease of the chore. They scale the first fifty stories in a mere fifteen minutes, as this time around there are no RATS buzzing through the vent shaft. By some stroke of luck they've all either been called to the surface levels for patrol or are stationed throughout the complex, giving the duo a clear path out of the substation.

Brutus passes Mace while they climb and looks back at him to say, "This is easy, when you said we were climbing two hundred stories I thought we were in for the usual punishment that comes with one of your ideas, but this is great. How long until you think we'll reach that elevator shaft?"

Mace looks up and says, "Not too long, another hundred and fifty stories or so."

Brutus looks down at the fifty stories they've already ascended which seemed easy at the time, he now peers up at the darkness that still lies ahead and suddenly regrets his words.

"It's a lot worse with fifty RATS phasing through while ya climb", Says Mace. "Consider yourself lucky."

Brutus replies, "Not that I'm complaining, but we don't exactly have a long standing streak of luck going here, so where exactly do you think they went?"

"I assume to look for us", says Mace hesitantly, as if not to jinx things.

They continue to climb and eventually Brutus falls a little behind Mace. Brutus starts to over think their situation and in turn he begins to have doubts.

He asks his friend, "So what do they know exactly?"

Mace replies, "Probably that we stole a substantial quantity of information off their system and killed several combat bots. I didn't even have time to shut down the console I was using so I guess it's safe to assume they know everything we've done."

"That's funny", Brutus responds, "I don't seem to remember that part of my day. I could swear I've spent the past several hours in an Aclysian playroom, but hey what do I know?"

Mace lets out an impulsive laugh.

Brutus sarcastically asks, "So were talking espionage and charges along those lines, right?"

"Among other things, likely treason", answers Mace. "We were here under a diplomatic shield, so violating their nation's security after being granted such a privilege will surely be considered a treasonous act. But don't worry about it, we got this."

"Who's worried", says Brutus with an unintended high-pitched tone as every nerve in his body seems to tense up in unison.

They pass the eighty-fourth sub-level and continue to talk as they climb. Brutus tends to become quite inquisitive when anxious.

"What will they do when they find the room empty?" He asks.

"They'll search it", Mace replies, "and soon realize that we didn't use the elevator to escape. We just need to hope they don't discover the vent shaft for a while. We wanna be out of this cage before that."

Brutus relaxes a little and they continue to advance. The two now remain silent as they progress hastily up the dark shaft. After about twenty more minutes of climbing they reach sub-level twelve.

Mace tells Brutus, "We're almost there."

He's incredibly relieved to hear this as Brutus is starting to feel significantly fatigued, which is adding to his already maxed out level of stress. Although small, scaling the compact levels of the Aclysian complex has taken it's toll on him.

As they continue to climb even higher, a light begins to develop underneath them. At first it is very dull, but it continues to grow in intensity and becomes extremely bright, extremely quickly.

Mace yells, "Hurry Brutus" and without even looking down his friend seems to get a burst of energy and catches up to Mace. It doesn't take him long, but within a matter seconds, the light is almost directly underneath the two. Mace glances over the object as it approaches and gets a glimpse of what there pursuer really is; it actually looks to be several RATS that use a coordinated light shield to blind and distract their enemies. Five of the small, hovering aircraft can be seen briefly, following the light shield up the shaft until the radiance becomes too bright and he can't make them out any longer.

The RATS slow down as they approach their targets and begin to hover just underneath the soldiers' feet. Brutus' hand almost loses his shallow grip, but he saves himself quickly and grabs back onto the side of the vent shaft. The brief disturbance is enough to cause the RATS focus to shift solely onto Brutus, leading Mace to instantly seize the opportunity to strike. He jumps across the vent shaft while covering his face from the blinding light and drops beneath the light shield's perimeter, opening his plasma staff while in the air. He clings to the wall and uncovers his face. Out of the RAT squadron's blinding light, he hurdles back across the shaft, moving in and out of sight while descending, with his Aclysian attackers now in desperate pursuit. Mace catches a glimpse of an Aclysian manually controlling one of the RATS, his small body crammed inside the tiny bot. He didn't even know that RATS could be manually piloted. The Aclysian looks quite strange to him without it's battle suit, so frail and petty. It trains its guns onto Mace who is quick to move out of its range and slashes two of the RATS in half, knocking them out of the air before making another leap across the shaft. As they fall to the bottom of what now seems like an endless tunnel, Brutus holds tight to the wall and swings his staff as far into the light as he can reach. He manages to pierce the generator of the powerful light shield and it pulsates as one of the RATS crashes hard into the side wall. The erratically hovering bot then spins out of control, bouncing off the narrow walls as it plummets. Lying directly in it's path, the other RATS still frantically pursue MACE down the shaft and are oblivious to their disabled comrade. Mace prepares for the collision, bracing himself tight to the wall and the out of control RAT soon catches up with the others. The three collide several times with the walls as well as each other, eventually dropping past Mace who slices one in half for good measure.

He laughs and yells up, "Who says we're not havin fun?"

Brutus replies, "Oh I know, I'm left blinded inside a dark vent shaft, things don't get much more jolly then this."

Mace looks up the shaft, "Well we destroyed those probes, but now they clearly know where we are. We're almost outta this shaft, I can see the accessway. Hopefully the Aclysians either won't remember or won' t think we can fit through it. Then after we get into the main elevator shaft we'll be home free."

They hustle up the last dozen stories of the sub-levels and quickly slide through the tight duct that takes them to the adjacent shaft. Once inside Mace leads the way and they hurry up towards the fifth floor where Mace had seen a power center during his earlier reconnaissance. As they pass by each floor Brutus can see Aclysian soldiers and RACS lining up in large formations to hunt them down.

When they approach the fifth floor Mace notices that the power center uses the elevator shaft as a network which wires and piping follow in order to leave the Aclysian complex altogether. This is necessary for the complex to receive and distribute power and information when needed. The fifth floor looks to be a closed hub, but there must be a full-service station nearby. They follow the network's hardware to it's highest area of concentration. Most of the pipes and wires relay to a single point on the twelfth floor, that must be the location of a main power station so they continue on their way.

When they get up to the twelfth floor, there appears to be no guards at all on this level. A further evaluation convinces the two that this is their best bet and they drop into the power station. Before jumping down, Brutus takes one more look into the elevator shaft where he sees a flood of RATS phasing through the walls of nearly every floor.

His eyes open up to twice the normal size as his feet hit the floor and he turns to Mace, "I think we better make this quick, they just stepped up their search."

Mace begins to survey the wire and piping network for a way out. Brutus tries to shake off the long climb by sitting down on the back of dual plasma generators housed inside a large coupling. Purple, orange, and turquoise colored plasma and chemical mixtures churn throughout the machine and simmer loudly. It's truly mesmerizing to watch the lava-lamp effect inside these massive, twelve foot tall plasma containers, the reactions seem volatile yet calculated, chaotic yet serene. Mace follows the network and finds a small pipeline that leads out of the fortress. They can follow it to more elevated areas of Aclysia, their best bet for finding a way off the planet. From there, they should be able to obtain a signal that can reach the UO.

He yells up to Brutus, "I got it! I've got our way out!"

As Brutus turns to look up he notices two fully suited Aclysian soldiers and two support RACS standing directly behind them. Apparently the pair's luck has run out, there was a security team stationed on this level after all.

One Aclysian yells to them, "How dare you disrespect our people you sad, pathetic fools! Kill them at once!"

Brutus, who is far closer to the Aclysian patrol than Mace, looks over to his friend bravely and says, "Go, I'll hold them off."

Brutus then lunges at the two Aclysian officers and the RACS back off. Based on their basic protocols they are trained never to apply lethal force while in close proximity to an Aclysian officer; theres too much of a risk that an Aclysian may be injured. The two Aclysian soldiers on the other hand immediately engage weapons of their own as two legs of their six-legged battle suits open to reveal a plasma chamber which resembles that of an extended plasma staff. Once they've taken a battle stance they walk on four back legs and fight with the additional two raised up, so they're pointing directly at the enemy, ready to impale. The Aclysians have adapted to and mastered this weapon with great proficiency, they do not allow their adversary to get near them while simultaneously attacking with a series of long-range, powerful blows. The two Aclysian officers attack Brutus viciously, having no issue with exploiting the odds. They swing their long cybernetic legs at him, but Brutus fights them off extremely well, showing impressive staff skills. He blocks their every blow and manages to avoid any dangerous contact with the battle suits. The Aclysians still don't relent once, every time one steps off the other proceeds to attack.

Mace doesn't even think twice about helping his partner, he's appreciative of Brutus' courage but could never leave his closest friend behind. He rushes back over, ignites his staff and jumps overtop one of the plasma generators. He clears the massive contraption with ease and attacks the two immobilized RACS from behind, partially decapitating them both with one swing of his staff. Mace then continues to attack aggressively by lunging towards the closest Aclysian officer with a flurry of quick swings and jabs. This catches the Aclysian off guard, and he is pushed back which separates them from Brutus and the second officer. Mace continues to duel with him as does Brutus with his adversary. After a brief tie-up, Mace pins one of the battle suit's weaponized legs to the generator and swiftly cuts his enemy in half while disabled. Then without a moments delay, Mace turns to help his friend, but is shocked by what he sees. Brutus has already killed the Aclysian soldier, who as they now look upon his corpse it can be seen that he was a Commander, and the soldier Mace battled was a lowly corporal.

Mace cheerfully says, "Good job buddy,"

Brutus smiles proudly and with an unfamiliar sincerity.

"Now let's get outta here."

With the Alcysians off their tails, the two cautiously crawl through the electrical pipeline. As they move along, the narrow tunnel widens out allowing them to stand up and walk freely. They cross several bulky groupings of bundled wires and grid couplings, careful not to disturb anything within the power grid which could lead to their detection. After a fairly descent walk they come to a small communications panel built into the tunnel itself, probably for use by workers and technicians. The two quickly juice it up and the system seems to work perfectly, a video link is opened but only a blank gray screen appears at first. Mace puts in their home coordinates to see if he can send a signal to Utopera, but it fails immediately. As he's trying to think of what the problem may be, he notices that someone is transmitting a blanket link to the planet for anyone to accept, this is what's blocking his transmission. He accepts the incoming message and is hit with a password screen, the screen reads, "The end to all we hold sacred". Mace recognizes the quote as one of Tagithus Hashin's most infamous, and also one of the Major's favorites. He immediately types in the answer, "Narel". The link connects and it's Major Parra.

"How ya doin boys?" he says with a smirk, "Don't you just love these supreme nations with their advanced diplomacy and such? So civil aren't they?"

Mace replies, "I must say, our holding room did exceed my expectations."

The Major laughs and responds, "I knew when I got pulled from an operations meeting with the Commanders that something was up. When the Aclysians told me you two were wanted for diplomatic injustices, as well as the acquisition of information damaging to Aclysian Security, I realized you must've found what we're looking for. Since being alerted of your fugitive status we sent in a cruiser and have been remotely monitoring all signals and frequencies surrounding Aclysia. I just got here myself, but you had us worried. What took you so long to pick up our call?"

Mace responds jokingly, "Sorry Major, you know how it is with all the cute Aclysian girls, not to mention the fine cuisine. We had to get one last taste of the sophisticated life."

The Major laughs eagerly at the blatant sarcasm.

"There's still no need to pat ourselves on the back just yet, can you pick us up?" He asks.

Parra answers, "Yea, not even the Commanders themselves could keep me from hearing what you've dug up now that we're this close. You're only a few kilometers from the end of that tunnel. We'll meet you in the center of an old Aclyisan sporting complex less than a mile north of there, it's been closed down and should shield our pick-up nicely."

"See you there Major", replies Mace.

He closes the video link then hurries to the end of the tunnel with Brutus. They run across several large clumpings of wire, careful to avoid dangerous gaps and faulty footings along the way. Once they exit the tunnel, the UO tandem runs out onto a platform atop one of the mid-levels of Aclysia. Massive buildings and immense superstructures surround them, while an entire metropolis also bustles beneath their feet. Constant air traffic speeds about high above, as the skyways are always packed on this planet.

The pair spots the massive sports complex up ahead, it stretches far beneath the current city level they travel upon, and extends at least another seventy Aclysian stories above their heads.

Mace says, "We should drop down a few levels, those main entrances will be our best option. The Major said it's closed down, so there shouldn't be much security."

Brutus nods in agreement and they continue on. The duo watches each other's back with vigilance, avoiding any civilian activity and using some impressive stealth to keep away from RAT squadrons sporadically patrolling the city. Lucky for them, typical Aclysian building design tends to use a surplus of pillars and overhangs, this provides great cover in situations like these. This architectural choice is another reason the Aclysian citizens were so hard to contain during the battle suit uprisings.

At last, they reach the sporting complex. The UO soldiers silently sneak passed a security center outside the building, careful to avoid the few Aclysian citizens present within the abandoned stadium. Inside, the view is even more impressive then on approach. The enormous, open-roofed stadium stretches on for hundreds of stories above their heads. It felt like being inside of a gigantic egg with one-quarter of it's top cut off. There is no sign of a UO pickup vessel, but Mace and Brutus rush through the bleachers to the center of the complex anyway.

As the two soldiers stand in the center of the futuristic-looking, worn down and tore up coliseum they stare to the sky, searching it for their getaway ride.

"Where are they?" Brutus asks, "I thought the retrieval ship would beat us here?"

"Probably just another minute, the Major won't let us down, be patient."

Seconds later, numerous Aclysian troops begin filing out of the inner workings of the stadium to surround Mace and Brutus. It seems they've been discovered and the tides of luck may truly be turning on the now unfortunate soldiers. As the bleachers fill with RACS and the two are effectively surrounded, a line of Aclysian tanks accompanied by dozens of soldiers and additional RACS enter through a large gate at the front of the arena, marching right up to the UO team where the lines finally halt.

Brutus says with a disheartened gasp, "You gotta be kidden me."

An Aclysian General who sits atop one of their over-sized war tanks yells out to them, "You have no were else to run our human guests. Now surrender yourselves and relinquish any information you've stolen from our databases. If you back down without a fight, I will contend that your extermination be administered painlessly."

Mace and Brutus ignite their staffs, when suddenly from above a UO A-CAM battleship appears. Hovering directly overtop the complex, the ship abruptly and fiercely attacks the unsuspecting Aclysian lines. Mace looks up to see the faint image of his support ship attacking when two zip lines are shot into the ground directly beside him. The Aclysians scatter to adjust their formation, but they don't have time. Plasma artillery fires from all sides of the hovering UO fortress while Mace and Brutus strap on their zip harnesses. The Aclysian forces frantically return fire to the sky, but are outmatched and quickly take significant losses. Once secured, Mace and Brutus are hoisted onto the ship within a matter of seconds. As soon as the soldiers are safely aboard, Major Parra orders the ship to immediately cease fire and ascend.

The Major greets his men, "Sorry to make it interesting, we had to wait until they threatened members of the UO before using hostile force. Politics I'm afraid."

"So you used us as bait", screeches Brutus, "Nice".

"You want to keep you're newly acquired information don't you? Now that we have a recording that shows the Aclysian Army threatening your lives, the Commanders won't even need to acknowledge their pleas of injustice. Beforehand, they never would have admitted to any hostility and likely would have painted you two as spies or rogue agents. Now, no matter what they say, with the footage we just shot the UO can't look like the bad guy."

Mace jumps in, "So I take it your gonna cut the video just before you started raining plasma all over that complex right?"

The Major gives a contained smile, "It may have incidentally stopped recording around that time. But that'd be purely coincidence of course."

Brutus laughs with them, "Oh of course."

As the battleship climbs it almost instantly becomes invisible once again, soon fully cloaked from most scanners. The Alcysian assault barely effected the goliath.

When the A-CAM battleship returns to Utopera and the infidisk that Mace had filled with data is finally analyzed, the evidence is indisputable. Mace and Brutus are commended for their work as well and both are awarded a galaxy medal, which is given to UO soldiers who perform exponentially well on an individual team mission. Mace and Brutus' credibility would skyrocket and finally Mace's theory would be taken seriously.

Although the mission was a success and the plot to take down the UO would now be viewed by all as a priority threat, there will still be a group of UO soldiers including certain Commanders that do not believe Narel is a part of it. They'll continue to dispute his very existence as if they were sleeping atop his grave each night. That's one of the largest problems when dealing with an organization containing the UO's amount of natural born leaders and the Verse's best trained soldiers, they're often exceedingly stubborn. It's starting to seem as though they won't be convinced otherwise until Mace, Major Parra, and the rest of their team can provide them with just that; either Narel's dead corpse or at the very least a public unmasking or appearance somewhere out in the Verse.

While the battleship returns our two soldiers home, Brutus retires to shower up and rest from the trying mission. Mace however decides to set up a video link with one of his oldest friends and mentors Centaro Abigus, a Centaur who is currently still fighting in the Centaur-Sirian War. Centaro is a General and fourth in line to become Primicus, the leader of the Centaurs. He and Mace became very close during Mace's time participating in that very same conflict. Despite the difference in heritage, Centaro considers this human his most exceptional pupil.

Mace awaits his mentor while sitting in front of the connecting video link, hoping to catch him in his quarters. Eventually, the Centaurian General's large head topped with spiraling, rounded horns suddenly appears on the screen and comes into focus. His serious stare lightens slightly at the sight of his student and friend.

"Greetings General", says Mace, "How are things looking on the warfront?"

Centaro smiles a little more, "Hello old friend, they're actually looking quite positive if you can believe it. We have the Sirian lines pushed back to the farthest positions in two decades. We've even managed to take back full occupation of Talinon."

"That's great news", Mace replies, the shock he feels leaking into his tone, "do you think there may finally be an end in sight?"

Centaro lets out a dull sigh, "Even with the way it's been going, I sincerely doubt it. This war won't end until an entire civilization sees extinction. Primicus Galenor believes that these past few years of failure will convince the Sirians to see reason and pull out, but I don't think he understands the level of foolish pride our enemy maintains. They would never withdraw from a conflict which they've sunk nearly an infinite supply of resources into, not to mention a century of their time. I believe that these beasts could be bankrupt and facing extinction, still they would continue to attack."

Mace gives a genuine sigh of his own, sincerely disheartened by the situation, "I'm truly sorry for the troubles of your people. A lot of us here wish there was more we could do."

"You've done your part", Centaro replies, "and although I hope desperately for an end to this bloodshed, I know that any further UO involvement could result in a Universal War and the casualties that outcome would produce are not worth the risk. This conflict is the unquestionable result of the Sirians' greed and aggression, nothing else. To be honest with you though, I don't even blame them anymore. The beasts that we fight today don't even have the chance to grow a conscience, they are simply bred into battle and they know no different. Not one Sirian fighting presently even knows why they hate us, they simply do, and thus they continue to fight. Beings of all races draw closer to one another through common nature, it's usually the more complicated issues of customs and culture that keep us apart. For them war is not an option, it's life. It has become their culture."

"I envy your stoicism", says Mace, "I doubt that I could evaluate my enemy so objectively, let alone be compassionate toward such a slanted perspective."

"Don't underestimate yourself my youth, I've seen you show compassion to enemies who were aiming to kill you just moments prior. You may make impulsive decisions, but you still manage to make them rationally. You're one of the most stoic beings I've ever encountered, and one of the few humans I've been proud to fight alongside."

Mace humbly replies, "Thank you Centaro".

"Now what's the reason for this call?" Asks Centaro, "You don't page me these days simply for a compliment session."

"You're right", says Mace, "As you know, I believe that Narel and several accomplice groups are behind a major threat to

the Verse. I've got some new information that leads me to believe
that the Sirians might be in on the plot as well. I know that with the
failures they've been experiencing out there it's unlikely that they'd
be involved in something this big, but have you seen
anything that may connect the two?"

Centaro thinks hard, but very briefly, then replies, "Well there
is one thing…."

Mace is too anxious to wait, "Well what is it?"

"A few of my scout ships have reported sightings of an
unidentified model of starship popping up in the back rows of the
Sirian lines. The reports have been coming in for nearly a year, but
I just recently received my first clear images of the vessels in
question and my first thought was that they look like an altered
version of the old Nexcin starships."

"That's interesting", Mace replies.

"Yes, interesting for us both", says Centaro, "At first I thought
it couldn't be, but with what you're saying I'm going to take a
harder look. I'll send you over the images, you can analyze them
for yourself. Let me know if you figure out anything more."

"Thanks", says Mace, "And good luck out there."

He goes to shut down the video link but Centaro stops him,
"Hold on a moment, can we speak for a bit longer?"

"Yea, no problem", he says, "I just have to get on this, that's
all. What's on your mind?"

Centaro takes a breathe, one much deeper than usual,
"Remember you're days training on Galaxo?"

Mace shakes his head yes and smiles as he recalls his time on
the Centaur training planet. Centaro continues, "From the first time
I met you I could sense that something was different about this
being; of all the pupils I've taught over all the decades, I've never
seen in any other what I saw in you. Defeating your combat
instructor on the first day of melee training, avoiding the level
seven ambush in the gauntlet, descending into the Joestra Trench
and emerging with a broken harness; honestly there's too many
impressive moments to remember them all. I'll never forget the day
I sent you out to face the Draka King. My fellow officers thought
I was a fool sending out our best new recruit alone on such an
exercise; many great Centaurs had died at the hands of
that king."

Centaro pauses a brief moment, attempting to gather his thoughts, "You see, unlike almost any other being I know of, you have this humble arrogance about yourself that combined with your combat skills makes you a remarkable soldier. Even against the bleakest of odds, you remain certain that you can find some way to survive and prevail. I mean I've come to know many; warriors, soldiers, mercenaries, and countless others who did not have one ounce of fear when faced with the proposition of death. They could stand right in front of their executioner, stare him in the eye, and smile as he pulls the trigger. Plenty have overcome the fear of death, that's nothing new, but there are very few who master it. They can look it in the eye as it faces them, yet they cannot escape it's grip and eventually the risky lifestyles they lead tend to catch up with them. You on the other hand have faced incredible odds and walked away without a scratch far too many times for it to just be luck or insanity. You explore every angle and avenue possible in order to lead yourself to survival or the accomplishment of your mission. I have no doubt that no matter how bad a situation gets, you would resist failure or death until the last breathe was ripped from your lungs."

Mace laughs humbily.

Centaro continues, his already serious voice dropping to an even more stern of a tone, "There is one other being who has come to convince me he possesses this overwhelming will to survive."

Mace quickly gives in to his curiosity, "Who?"

"Narel of course", replies Centaro.

Mace gives him a confused stare, "Was that an insult or a compliment?"

"Merely an observation my friend. I know that I'm lucky to have trained and fought alongside you. I may not even be here today if it weren't for you, but you must be careful young warrior. Wisdom is the path to true power and in order to receive and retain such knowledge one must follow their path with patience and forethought. You are so quick to be the mediator and jump from one conflict to another, you decrease even the greatest soldier's chance of survival. You need to hold onto your civilian life; family, friends, your home. It's what keeps a warrior grounded, and his vision clear."

Mace becomes frustrated, "Is there a point to this? I live my civilian life in my mind everyday and I could never forget it. I miss them every second, but I can't go back to that until I can make things right! I follow trouble because I do all that I can to stop it! And because I care enough to do so, no one else seems to. I thought if anyone would understand that it'd be you."

"I do have a point", says Centaro, as sincere and concerned as he can sound, "If you're correct about Narel, which I believe you are, then he is far, far ahead of you. He's not the impulsive warlord he once was. That dark soul was always brilliant, he's only recently grown wise. Proceed with caution, as I believe that your path is about get much more difficult and your journey is long from over."

Mace says, "What are you talking about? Do you know something?"

Centaro replies, "Only that if he is back, you are going to have to be the one who stops him. No one else within the UO or anywhere for that matter has the skill set to kill him now, nobody but you. Not only is he a great warrior, he has always been just as committed to survival as you and over the ages has become infinitely wise. The entire universe has feared him before, so what do you think they'll do now? I need to leave you with that, meditate on it, and keep in mind that every situation you experience in life is training. Remember all, interpret all. Goodbye my friend."

They both shut down the video link and Mace sits back, pondering Centaro's words.

Far away from Utopera, within a distant, reclusive sector of the Verse; a large, shadowy figure stares out the window of his starship, looking into the vast nothingness of space that surrounds him.

A powerful warlord named Demos Bellerus comes walking into the room, looking as determined as one individual could. Demos is a ruthless Renondin warrior and one of the most feared beings alive. He is known throughout the Verse for his combat abilities as well as his general disregard for civilian life. Renondins are short, usually only around five feet tall, but they are one of the strongest races in the Verse pound for pound. Their entire civilization destroyed itself through a violent period of power struggle and unrelenting civil war.

The dark figure speaks without even turning to his visitor, "What is it Demos, you look discouraged?"

Demos, trying to hide the aggravation in his voice replies, "The UO has found an infidisk with the allocation codes on it."

"Yes, I know", the figure responds.

"Well', says Demos, "Did you know that they've used the code to unlock the Aclysia files. Inventories, objectives, schematic breakdowns; they have it all."

The figure turns to reveal a being unlike any other in the Verse. This creature, with shoulders so wide that they stretch out to nearly the equivalent of his eight feet in height, had a stature and build that is truly one of a kind.

"They have nothing, simply numbers and maps." He says, seemingly without care. "The Org will be heavily implicated as we had planned, while the Sirians remain protected by the shroud of the hundred year war. As for us, the UO couldn't stop me now if I landed atop one of their fortresses bound and unconscious."

Demos replies, "But Lord Nare…."

He is interrupted abruptly, "But nothing General Bellerus, this plan has been in development since before your birth and there is not one possible cause for which it will be rushed. The UO is no threat at this stage, I know their every action before they do."

He pauses for a moment but raises his hand slightly, brazenly signaling Demos not to speak, "As for the Org, they've more than served their purpose, kill every member that could have any information detrimental to my army. Cut off any remaining remnants of the Organization from all further funding and let them fend for themselves. The resulting splinter gangs that form and struggle to survive will create crime waves which will hinder and scatter the UO even further. It won't be much longer now. We only have one more obstacle left before the take over; shift the focus of all our efforts to ending the Sirian's troubles. Once the Centaurs are out of the way, we can help the Sirian Army rebuild at an advanced rate and once their military is back to at least seventy five percent we will put the final stage into effect. Then we will attack, and within one day's time Utopera will be destroyed and the Universe will be ours! Vindication will come soon, my disciple."

As for the data found on Mace's infidisk, it revealed many new leads and tons of information so it gave the UO team a lot of work to do. As they had predicted Narel's plan was advanced, detailed, and well-designed; some major pressure would need to be applied in order to get him out of hiding and into custody.

Lost Asteroid

The next segment of our story begins in 2524, just as Mace, Brutus, and the rest of the Universal Order finish up their dissemblance campaign against Org terrorists operating throughout the Verse. After the UO decoded all of the information stored on the Valeena infidisk, courtesy of the Aclysians, hundreds of locations used by the Org and other conspirators were exposed. After careful analysis and planning, the UO began a massive operation designed to infiltrate the Org's ranks. It took several years, but they have penetrated the universal crime syndicate through and through; they're now in the final stages of dismantling the few scant remnants of the once universe-encompassing criminal organization.

Thirty-three different Org leaders have fallen over the past four years, five killed by the UO and twenty-eight are of assumed to have been assassinated by disgruntled Org members. Another thirty thousand beings associated with the Org have either been captured or killed over the three year campaign. The Org is so well spread that it is unlikely they'll ever be eradicated from the Verse entirely, but all in all they are no longer considered a threat, the UO's concern has shifted solely to Narel who has still not been substantially affected by their pursuit. The hunt is finally on however; Mace, Brutus, and hundreds of other UO teams are checking every sector of the Verse in search of the infamous king of all warlords.

Brutus has received some down time after he and Mace's most recent accomplishment, stopping thirty terrorists attempting to bomb a multi-level shopping complex on Validagah, and capturing the majority of them alive. One was even a Nexcin believed to be coordinating the attack, quite the achievement even for these two. Now, Brutus is happy to be returning to Earth once again, he's become more than homesick over this long operation.

Its been over a year since his last visit and he can't wait to be on his way. Mace on the other hand has no plans of taking a break, he's already following up leads provided by his new prisoners, although they haven't yet been able to get any information out of the lone Nexcin. The retched-smelling pawn laughed in the faces of his UO captors, spit in their eyes as his wounds were pressured, and proclaimed that Narel was the one true ruler of the Verse. To say the least, he doesn't seem to be a very promising lead.

Brutus asks Mace to return home with him once again but he doesn't push. Mace refuses as always, politely telling Brutus, "Send my best wishes to everyone".

Brutus responds, "They don't want your praise, they want to see you."

Mace snaps back, "I can't Brutus, you know that. Not yet."

Mace then grabs his bag with a hostile grip and storms out, headed straight for his fighter.

As he leaves Brutus yells out, "That's right, fearless Mace Crimson runs again from the only thing he's truly scared of….home!"

The distraught and possibly homesick Mace continues storming down the hall and through the docking station straight onto his ship. He blasts off for the mission without saying goodbye to anybody else; he doesn't even clear his launch with the docking operator who yells through Mace's com board, "You're not clear! You're not clear!"

The frantic calls are ignored by the emotional soldier, who's obviously been effected by his friend's departure to their home, more so than he's ever shown before. Crimson turns his boosters to full blast once he's clear of the gates, making it evident that he wants to get far away as fast as he can. The ship rattles and shakes slightly more than normal, this causes him to run a general scan of his systems. Shortly after, everything comes back fine and Mace sits back in his chair, drifting into deep thought.

After a few minutes, while still feeling the sting of Brutus' words, he notices a change in color ahead of his ship. A bright, glowing light that seems to go through all the shades of the spectrum in an incredibly vibrant display of magnificence, flashes right before the soldier's eyes and lies directly within his flight path. The sight doesn't last long, as he is suddenly knocked off his feet and drops to the floor unconscious. As he lies there helpless, the fighter begins to shake once again, this time with much greater turbulence, and it doesn't seem to cease.

Back on Utopera, Brutus heads over to the dining hall and eats some Gulan, a Utoperan cuisine that is said to taste a hundred times better than the finest steaks on Earth or Mars, however it comes from a disgusting-looking creature. He's filling up on his favorite dish one last time before the intensely long trip home. He sits and eats with Arilla as well as two Sergeants; Wellit and Cunnins, an Artilonian and a Tringalean respectively, along with two privates, Rallo And Lena, both of whom are Balons.

Brutus quietly enjoys his meal as the group talks about several issues, including the increases in resource pricing as well as the instability many solar systems have been experiencing.

Sergeant Cunnins comments on the micromanaging of UO soldiers now adays. He's served the UO for fifty three years so he understands the change better than most.

"It never used to be like this" he says as he leans back in his chair, "I got pulled from my last mission because I didn't clear a meeting with the Trinada Guard during a treaty signing over there. I spent twenty-two cycles persuading both groups to cease fire under my command, then they go and pull me off the operation over some bureaucratic nonsense. Afterward everyone's left wondering why the fighting starts again less than a cycle after my departure. I feel like soon we'll reach the point where I'm gonna have to seek permission from the council to clear my bowels."

"Or to get some alone time with the wife", Rolla adds.

Arilla sarcastically replies, "Your wife could only wish to be so lucky".

They all share a laugh and continue with the small talk, mostly the privates yammering back and forth, until Arilla says to Brutus, "So let me ask you something B, does Mace ever visit home?"

The rest of the group turns their attention to Brutus, as its long been wondered by the majority of his peers why Mace doesn't return home, or even speak of it for that matter.

Brutus thinks for a moment, seeming as though he's unsure whether or not he should even answer the question. "Something happened", he says, "it forced him to leave and scarred him so bad he can't go back."

Private Lena anxiously jumps in, "Well what happened?"

Brutus answers her with only a stern look. Arilla can tell this is a touchy subject and redirects the conversation, "Well, are you happy to be making the trip, it's been a while now?"

"Of course", exclaims Brutus, "I've been itchin to go for months. We've been so consumed with leads lately, I haven't been able to schedule a trip back for over a year. Once I do get back there, I really don't know how I'm gonna be able to leave everyone this time."

Private Rallo adds, "That's what I thought when I was granted my last leave. Somehow after a week back home I remembered why I came out here to begin with."

Brutus laughs and says, "Not me, my family's always been the most important thing I have and I've never been away from them this much, these past few years have really been rough with all the chaos around here."

Sergeant Wellit joins the conversation, "If your such a family man Callous, then what brought you into the UO to begin with? We're not exactly a family friendly employer, I mean even officers aren't usually allowed to move more than their wives and children to Utopera."

Brutus replies, "Mace is the closest family I've got, always has been. I couldn't let him come out here completely alone, while I'm back there with everyone else. Back home they all have each other, but out here Mace would have no one. I know that probably didn't matter much to him, he's never been afraid to stand alone, but I wouldn't have been able to live with it. He's closer than a brother to me, I could never abandon him."

Arilla mocks Brutus' new found sentimental side, "Aw, maybe you shoulda told him about about all these feelings and emotions before he left."

Brutus pushes his tray towards her, pretending as though he's going to spill it onto Arilla's lap. He catches the tray at the last second and joins in a laugh.

She then says, "In all seriousness, that's one of the most noble things I've ever heard. For the record, I think he needs you. He'll never show it, but he does."

As Brutus finishes up he tells the group, "Well I'm off, my shuttle leaves in a half hour."

He hugs his friends goodbye and as the overworked soldier throws out his tray, a frantic UO recruit can be seen running across the lounge. The undersized soldier-in-training sprints up to a group of Commanders who sit at a distant table. The recruit is out of breathe and gasps as he loudly blurts out, "Sergeant Crimson's tracking beacon disappeared." He takes a few more deep breathes. Brutus begins moving closer so he can hear more clearly. He yells, "Speak boy!"

The recruit replies, "We have no idea what happened, all attempts to contact the ship or any of it's instruments since his tracker went out have been useless. Our technicians can't tell if it's interference, an elaborate jamming system, or something else.

"What else", asks Arilla, as all the soldiers have now gathered around.

The recruit hesitantly replies, "It seems possible that the ship may have been lost all together; an elaborate pirate attack or a rogue comet perhaps."

The Commanders get up to leave and Brutus hustles ahead of them. He rushes to the research archives, a frequent daytime home of Major Parra. There, he runs into Lieutenant Lang.

"Gil, where's the Major? Mace is in trouble."

Lang turns to him and is quick to answer, "I know, a messenger just pulled the Major out of here for an emergency gathering in the assembly hall."

"Then why are you still here" Brutus says, "let's go."

"High ranking officials only, unless you got an invite you're not welcome. Guess we're gonna have to wait."

Brutus isn't about to be left in the dark while his friend is lost in space. He sprints off, running through the calm halls of the UO headquarters as quickly as he can racing towards the council room. He maneuvers sharply through the narrow alleys created by traffic within the base as well as other obstacles, obliviously disrupting the otherwise peaceful atmosphere of Utopera.

Out of breathe and sweating, Brutus crashes through the chamber doors with an outrageous clang as his armor collides with the sturdy alloy frame. The session, which is led by several commanders and already in progress, stops with quite an awkward pause as perhaps every officer in the large auditorium turns around and peers back at Brutus.

He apologizes, "Sorry for the intrusion, proceed commanders".

Five Commanders sit at an elevated, C-shaped table in front of the large room. Surprisingly, as Brutus is not invited nor technically aloud to be present at the gathering, the meeting continues with Commander Ziel picking up where she'd left off, "If his ship disappeared then the most likely conclusion is that Sergeant Crimson is dead."

Major Parra speaks out, "It's outrageous to assume him deceased simply because we lost his signal. This is an experienced officer with more commendations than most sitting in this room or even upon that podium; he could be shipwrecked, stranded in space, or even held hostage for all we know. It's well understood that
Mace is integral to our most important objective at the moment."

Commander Ziel says, "Those possibilites are all unlikely, a tracking beacon cannot be shut off or dismantled. The only way it would stop transmitting is if it were destroyed. The bottom line is that we're talking about one soldier out there and we don't have the manpower to…"

Commander Quita jumps in, "Before we turn this into a debate over whether or not Lieutenant Crimson is worth searching for, because as we all know every soldier on this planet is worth at least that much, let's discuss exactly why we're really here. Why half of the UO's top officials have been called in to a meeting to reach a decision that would normally have been left up to the pair of Commanders currently on duty. Since I happened to be one of those Commanders, I'll tell you why."

He calmly takes a drink from a half empty glass that sits in front of him. The entire assembly hall remains silent as he drinks, a sign of the respect Quita commands. He finishes his drink and replaces the glass before continuing.

"The reason you've all been taken from your families or dragged from your work is because the situation at hand is much more perplexing than first appearances dictate and needs the attention of our collective minds. What took place is unprecedented to say the least, you see Lieutenant Crimson left the third squadron docking bay less than ninety minutes ago. Within an hour of travel, radus had tracked and recorded his journey immaculately. He cruised through the first three sectors at full throttle with go readings from every system and not a single mechanical failure. Hasty and a little odd to travel at such high speeds so rapidly, but likely just a sign that Crimson was anxious to get on his way."

Brutus feels guilty, as he knows that he's likely the reason for Mace's haste.

"At this time, his instruments show a large, but instantaneous power spike upon entering his fourth sector of travel, 116-B. He continued on at full thrust until about mid-way through the sector when his beacon suddenly disappears from the Verse. We have positive readings from every scanner active at the time and that beacon doesn't show up on a single one, meaning it was gone."

Commander Quita pauses, but no one in the crowd gives much reaction. The truth is, any one of a million occurrences could have caused Mace to crash and permanently disable his beacon.

The Commander continues, "None of you seem as shocked as I, but the reason this is so bothersome is because a mere three seconds later, Lieutenant Crimson's beacon appears six zones away, in 186, before vanishing again after just two seconds more."

An Abrupt onslaught of chatter and confusion overtakes the room. The officer's packed within the hall begin acting like a crowd of miscreants; speaking loudly, out of turn, and overtop of one another. The rambling soon escalates like a cafeteria full of school children. They had went from misinformed and unconcerned to skeptical, irrational, and confused from this one statement.

Most find it hard to believe that a ship could simply disappear and reappear like that, no UO fighter could be fitted with a wormhole generator it was too small to sustain the force. The standard transmitter on any sanctioned UO fighter is glitch-less, and no malfunction using the current model has ever occurred. Other officers are intrigued, and immediately interested in finding out what caused such an anomaly. There is no other known way to skip from one zone to another, the entire situation just doesn't seem plausible. The only logical explanation is that some greater force or plot is at work. The thought of Narel jumps into the minds of many, but none dare mention the notion.

A gathering of officers often implies a gathering of strong-minded individuals, as they wouldn't have made it to such a distinction without this trait. As a result, compromise is not reached as often as may be beneficial because no leader out there likes to concede his point, no matter how persuasive the other side may be.

The rambling continues for a bit until Commander Quita intervenes, "It's obvious that this matter requires some attention", he shouts out. Again the respect he's earned quiets the room fairly quickly. "Now the question is, what's to be done? We are already spread thin throughout the Verse, if we pull any details off their assignments, significant progress may be lost. Also, were we to send a fleet from Utopera it would need to be extremely small. We're already far too close to the minimum numbers needed to protect the Capitol, a rule that cannot be bent during times such as these."

Commander Lozika speaks up, "We need to at least send a survey team to analyze the situation, who knows what could've happened out there? We need to investigate for safety concerns at the very least."

Commander Blenko steps in, "I disagree, we should wait and see if a distress signal or retrieval message is sent out. From what I hear Sergeant Crimson is quite resourceful, if he's alive he'll probably find a way to contact us. He's likely the only one who can fill us in on exactly what's happened. It could even be an elaborate trap set by enemies of the UO, these times warrant such a concern."

Major Parra raises up and Commander Quita points to him, permitting the Major to speak, "Waiting would be foolish, if something happened out there any evidence will have drifted over a sector away by the time we assemble a team."

Commander Ziel is quick to retake her position against the Major, "Protecting Utopera is and always will be the primary objective of the UO, it can be compromised for nothing."

"Yes I know" The Major replies, "That's why I propose sending a small fleet, larger than a survey team, but just enough to thoroughly evaluate the situation and perform a quick sweep of the sector."

Commander Gura, who has been silent thus far speaks up, clearing his throat before saying, "I agree, at least a small search and recovery team must be sent."

With Commanders Lozika, Gura, and Quita all agreeing, the majority of active Commanders was in favor of a search fleet.

"Thank you commanders", The major says, "I'll assemble a team right away".

"That won't be necessary Major", says Commander Ziel, "if a team is going to be sent, I'll take the liberty of forming it."

At this point Brutus stands up without hesitation and says, "Excuse me Commanders, but if anyone is going to be sent to uncover the truth behind this situation, I am without a doubt the best soldier in this room for the job."

Commander Ziel peers out at Brutus, "Excuse me..." she squints as if struggling to identify his rank, "Sergeant, I will appoint the fleet myself and I assure you that they'll be perfectly capable."

Major Parra attempts to speak, but Brutus talks over him pleading to the Commanders, "Mace is my partner and my best friend, I've learned everything I know from him and I can think more like him than any one of you. If anybody can find him it'll be me, and when I do you can discover exactly happened to his ship."

Commander Ziel responds, now yelling, "Sergeant Tailkon will lead the..."

"No Commander", Quita asserts, "Initiative and drive are exactly the prerequisites for a mission such as this. Sergeant Tailkon can accompany the fleet if that will please you, but Sergeant Callous will lead the mission."

Ziel stands down to Quita once again and Quita continues.

"They will venture to the second sight coordinates, the spot where the beacon appeared only briefly. The search party will be given a cruiser with warp generator, due to the time factor. The cruiser will also carry a squadron of search and retrieval vessels as well as rescue and surveillance equipment. A secondary scanning and detection team will be sent to the first site in order to try and pick up on any evidence left floating in space. The mission will commence as soon as your fleet is ready, good luck Sergeant."

Callous gives a stern smile to the Commander and walks out.

Major Parra catches up to him, "I don't know where that came from Callous, but you couldn't of picked a better time to speak up. You need to find Mace, everything we've worked for is lost without him."

Brutus confidently says only two words, "I will" and heads towards his quarters to prepare for departure.

Over in zone 186 Mace awakens to the sounds and heat of his ship making an atmospheric breach. As he comes to, all the disoriented soldier can see is a mesmerizing display of gray and purple swirling clouds covering a small, dark world. He tries to snap himself out of his barely conscious state, but as the ship propels to the ground with magnanimous force, spinning and diving out of control, there's little the soldier Mace can do. He attempts to open all flaps and stabilize the fighter, pulling the levers with all his might. The craft cant be controlled however and several flaps are ripped off instantly; a few others hold up but they don't seem to be much help. All boosters have been disabled and most of his onboard computer systems are barely responding. No matter how hard Mace fights with the helm he can't regain control of the ship, the small half-moon shaped wheel simply won't budge. A screeching noise made by the fighter's resistance as it enters the atmosphere is deafening and drowns out all other sound entirely; picking up in intensity as the ship picks up speed. Not much can be seen past the cloud line, and as he drops through the atmosphere the unfortunate soldier's not exactly sure what he's even barreling into. Suddenly, the ship breaks free from the clouds to an astonishing sight; a beautiful world of forests, mountains, glistening bodies of water, and many unknown wonders appear before him. Beneath the thick and mysterious clouds of this place, such incredible beauty is hidden. Mace truly could not believe his eyes as he sat back in his seat, his body almost appearing as though it went completely relaxed. The bewildered soldier had no last minute idea that could save him this time, he simply sat there and gazed in amazement. Without fear, he admired this unknown world during what would almost certainly be his final moments.

As the ship dropped closer and closer, the outline of a bi-pedal being can be seen standing on the surface of the unknown world, appearing to be within a direct flight path of the fighter. The rejuvenated soldier perks back up and frantically tries to adjust the controls, even a slight alteration could shift the impact site enough to save this foolish creature. Unfortunately, and to the disappointment of Mace, the flight controls remain locked it would seem that the fighter's trajectory is final. Suddenly, it felt as though things were slowing down, like the ship was decelerating, but seconds later it smashes into the planet...all air-bags and safety mechanisms deploy and Mace is knocked unconscious once again.

He is out for several minutes before awakening unharmed, strewn out across the ground several feet from his ship. The confused soldier sits up and looks around to see nothing, just a view that's both spectacular and eerie simultaneously. He lays amongst a tropical paradise, with beaches surrounding him and an oasis just off in the distance, the only trees that stand are palms and galas just at the water's edge. The strange part is that upon his rapid descent, Mace saw vast plains and meadows running beneath him. Also, off in the distance he can see soaring mountaintops or what perhaps may even be massive snow-covered glaciers. As he tries to analyze each direction surrounding him, the traveled UO lieutenant can't even identify some of the terrain he witnesses. A majority of it appears to be thick with vegetation, but in some places the varieties seemed unimaginable. None of this made sense, and neither did the fact that Mace was unharmed and lying next to the ship instead of being crushed inside of it. He continues to puzzle as he picks himself up off the ground. As the soldier looks over to his fighter, it too appears completely undamaged from the crash. As he walks closer there doesn't appear to be a scratch on it, but as he reaches the nose of the ship he peers upon two, decent sized imprints pressed deeply into the front cap.

As he looks closer, inspecting the peculiar dents, the soldier thinks to himself, "what could be strong enough to smash in the front of a ship like this? Even stranger, what stopped the ship from crashing, at all. Me and it should be lining the bottom of a crater right now?"

He begins to check the ship for damages, along with any supplies that may be used. While searching, he continues to puzzle over what exactly is happening.

Off in a distant part of the Verse, a Nexcin Lieutenant kneels before his leader, whose back is turned to the officer. They are on the bridge of a grand Nexcin starship, about a dozen pilots surround the two as they stand upon an elevated central bridge. The dimly lit bridge is almost as dark as the empty space that sits directly outside it. This is because all of Narel's starships and most other vessels within the Nexcin fleet do not contain any traditional form of lighting. Instead, some of the excess plasma which flows through the ship's engines while active is pumped into veins throughout the halls and chambers of each craft. This saves energy created by the engines by using a natural byproduct to produce light, rather than wasting energy to power them. The surplus energy is converted into increased output and extra thrust when his fleets are in battle, a major advantage to the Nexcins during interstellar conflicts.

The once Artilonian officer pauses for a moment, with no acknowledgement from his leader, then speaks "We've received word from Lustrum my lord."

Narel turns to face his follower, "And?"

"The resistance there remains significant, Oreg's nineteenth battalion is nearly depleted with little progress to show. We've lost countless soldiers over the past few cycles and several years worth of supplies all in vein."

Narel's forces usually defeat an enemy of average or below average intelligence within a matter of days, not full cycles. Needless to say, the warlord is outraged at such an impediment.

"That planet is only home to a few primitive indigenous species!" Exclaims Narel, "how can they be defeating my army?"

The Nexcin doesn't seem intimidated by his leader, yet he is still somewhat reluctant to answer, "The Beluans and their beasts of war have decimated our infantry as well as vehicles with crude, yet vicious partisan tactics. Although the race itself is fairly primitive, their astounding knowledge of the home terrain has made them nearly unconquerable."

"Unconquerable?" says Narel as his discontent grows considerably, "really Lieutenant?"

He walks past his subordinate and peers out a large starship window, his mind trained deep in thought. After just a few moments he spins around slowly and breaks the silence.

"I haven't the time for these feeble setbacks, I need that planet for strategic positioning and I need it now. Prepare a fighter for my departure, I'll take care of this problem myself."

The Lieutenant wisely agrees, "Yes my lord, right away. How many reinforcements do you wish to accompany you?"

Narel suddenly wears a fossilized smile, "I said I was going myself Lieutenant, there won't be any need for additional reinforcements. Prepare my ship and keep the fleet on standby until my return."

The Lieutenant gives a small bow, graciously accepting his orders before leaving Narel's chamber to relay the commands.

Back on the asteroid Mace begins to marvel at the wondrous sights surrounding him as he continues to inspect his ship, which oddly enough seems to be in fine working order. The control systems and all instruments power up without malfunction and the astounded soldier plans to leave as soon as the boosters warm back up. He leans forward to check on how many flaps remain usable. He drops his head under the main controls when out of the corner of his eye he notices something moving toward him, bolting across the desert with great speed. As it glides across the open, beach-like terrain the being can be seen coming from afar, yet within seconds the object somehow travels what must be several miles and in almost no time reaches Mace sliding to a halt just a few feet from the ship, kicking a wave of sand up into the air as he comes to a stop. It is a single being, no craft or fancy propulsion suit, just a large, seasoned-looking warrior wearing little armor. As Mace freezes, staring in silence for a moment, it dawns on him that he's looking at the same being which stood unflinchingly inside the path of his ship while crashing. No words are exchanged as the being stares back at Mace for a bit, gazing at him as though he were trying to read into his soul. The being begins to step closer to the UO fighter.

Mace jumps out of the ship and backs away from the unknown creature as he pulls out his plasma staff.

The large gray being looks over Mace and smiles sarcastically; he then lifts his hand slightly and pulls the plasma staff right from the soldier's grip without ever touching it. It appears as though the creature can use telekinesis with relative ease, Mace had never seen such an effortless display. The being then raises his other hand and knocks Mace's feet out from under him, dropping the soldier to the ground. While Mace lies on his back, powerless to the alien, it rips apart his plasma staff in mid-air, dissembling the weapon into dozens of pieces. The spear-like tips of the staff slide off first, popped free from their welded seal without the faintest sound. Next the plasma chambers are opened up and unentwined, all remaining plasma dissipates away to nothing. The dismantling continues rapidly and after a short time the staff has been broken down to its smallest components. All the parts and pieces remain suspended above the ground just in front of Mace for a few moments; never before had the veteran soldier felt so helpless. Then abruptly, the pieces are cast off with unparalleled force, launching out in all different directions until vanishing into oblivion.

The mysterious being speaks, "There are no weapons allowed here my friend."

Mace replies after a brief pause, "And where exactly is here?"

"Hard to say precisely", the being answers, "the natives who lived here long ago believed this was the center of the Universe. Always moving, unaffected by time and space, it can be both anywhere...and nowhere."

Mace has dealt with some strange characters over the years, some with even stranger beliefs, but this guy looks like he might take the cake. He skeptically responds, "Right, so who are you? How did you do that to my staff and how do you move so fast?"

"Who I am lost relevance long ago", it replies, speaking with an underlying sense of wisdom. "I was once the powerful leader of billions of followers, but after numerous failures and foolish decisions I was exiled here for all of eternity."

Mace impulsively asks, "Why were you exiled?"

"It is not important", the being snaps back, "your arrival here is solely where your concerns should lie."

Mace questions this, "What does my arrival have to do with anything? I crashed here by accident, believe me it was not by choice."

The being replies with certainty in his voice, "It may not have been your choice, but I assure that you did not end up here by accident. You see there are certain rules to this place, rules that I must abide by if I ever want to be relinquished from my term. Rules that you must abide by now that you've come."

"You don't understand", says Mace impatiently, "I can't deal with this now, I have an important mission and I need to get back on my path as quickly as possible. Please just let me be on my way."

"It's you who doesn't understand", he replies, "I am the caretaker of this sanctuary and I'm required a fight to the death with any being I encounter here. I sincerely apologize, but I must uphold this stipulation without personal judgment or exception."

Mace contemplates for a second, "Well you could have killed me before I even woke up from the crash, or from what I gather, you stopped my ship from crashing all together. So why not just let me barrel into the planet if that's what would have appeased your rules?"

"That's not how it works", the being calmly responds, "you are to be given a time of two weeks here, time in which you may better adapt and adjust to your surroundings. The properties of this place are unlike that of any other in the Verse; study them, understand them, and perhaps you'll survive. After your time is up, we will meet once again and have our battle."

Mace looks down for an instant, appearing to bow in dismay. Then suddenly, he kicks a plumb of sand at the being and lunges back toward his ship, attempting to spring for a speedy escape. In less than an instant the being moves in front of Mace then telekinetically tosses him aside, rolling the soldier helplessly onto a small dune. The creature then moves a few feet closer to Mace's ship and turns his focus to the sands beneath the UO fighter. Mace can only watch as the sands shift and swirl as if it were a whirlpool in an ocean and his ship begins to get sucked into the ground. It descends quite rapidly, and Mace barely has time to yell out, "Stop, fight me now!" He is helpless to move as the mysterious caretaker somehow manages to keep the soldier's joints locked into place. Within a matter of minutes, only the very tip of his ship remains visible as the vessel becomes submerged beneath tons of sand.

The mysterious being then says, "Do not look at this in a negative way, you have been chosen soldier. This utopia is an incredible place and you are one of only a few beings in the history of the Verse who shall see it."

It then bends down and places its large, gray hand to the ground, slowly closing both eyes. "Feel the raw energy here; as it dances between the grains of sand, flows in harmony through the rivers, wraps like a maze around the canyons, passes seamlessly through your very body without the slightest resistance, circles the asteroid, and echoes it's presence through every dimension."

He opens his eyes back up and stands once again, "Embrace your surroundings in the time to come, feel the untainted energy of this place, as if you hope to defeat me you'll need to discover more than just the beauty of this special world."

Mace replies, "If you're going to kill me just do it now. I don't have time for these games."

The being gives Mace another sarcastic smile and like a flash is gone, running with blazing speed off into the distance. As his joints loosen up, and he regains movement, Mace retrieves survival gear that was pulled from the ship before it's impromptu burial and prepares to set up camp. As he hears a few disturbing calls from the surrounding wildlife, the soldier decides to search the terrain for a more suitable, less open place to spend the night.

He first marches to the oasis he'd noticed earlier and tests the water with a sanitation gauge built into his armor, it's confirmed to be clean and drinkable. He gathers as much as he can carry and sets off, trekking towards some of the colorful terrains up ahead. As he moves across the tropical, desert-like lands the only change in elevation comes from dunes which are scattered about endlessly. A majority of the larger dunes look to have formed based on the wind cycles, likely over very long stints of time. Some others however seem to be artificial, made by some sort of life form as a means of tunneling beneath the desert floor. These mounds are much more prevalent in some areas than others and Mace decides it would be most wise to stay away from them. After walking several miles through the sand, he encounters a transitional area that provides a long, flat, neutral break of land that branches off into several different climate zones. This neutral terrain varies in color, but appears to remain flat and lifeless in all directions. Sometimes snow covered, others with lava flowing just underneath the surface; this barrier region seems to be present between all visible climate zones, keeping them separate and distinct. It almost looks like a grid of specially engineered territories, but it was much too perfect to be artificial. No terraforming he had ever known could produce so many diverse climates with such an impeccable efficiency. It had to be natural, but how?

The tired soldier analyzes his options. Directly in front of him lies a large, jagged volcano that appears to be currently active. As he made his way across the extensive desert-like landscape, some seismic activity could be felt which intensified as his proximity to the lava-filled mountain drew closer. Obviously this path would be a poor choice. Off to his right, Mace sees a vast arctic region, one that stretches out much farther than his eyes can see. The area is hill covered, and Mace struggles to decipher whether or not the protruding, often pointed hilltops are just that, or if perhaps they're glaciers floating atop a frozen sea. Either way, this path does not look very promising. His best option is definitely to his left; here a thick and vibrant forest climbs right up to the edge of the afore mentioned neutral area. The territory looks to be teeming with life, which also means it should be quite passable. As he looks further left he can see yet another option, a descending slope that leads into a mineral wasteland of some sort. The rocky landscape swirls with colors of blue, silver, black, gray, brown, red and white; looking similar to a finely created marble surface with striking detail and design. The slope leads into a massive quarry of the eroded and naturally refined minerals that looks to have developed over several millennium. Quite breathtaking, but this final option would be difficult to reach due to the treacherous slope that lies before it; it would in turn be exceedingly easy to hike once he got there, but once again Mace would be left out in the open. He chooses to enter the thick forest at his near left, and shortly after begins to make his way into the mysterious jungle.

Back on Utopera, Commander Quita has been cornered by several other UO commanders who are disturbed by the events that took place earlier, as Brutus was given permission to lead Mace's rescue mission. Quita is looking over various defense post schematics via a three dimensional terminal located in the Council Archive Hall. Commander's Ziel, Blenko, and Tilk enter and Ziel as usual is the first to speak.

"May we have a moment Commander?"

Quita turns to his peers, "Of course, although I know why you're here."

Ziel adamantly replies, "I'm sure you do, we just saw a mere Sergeant impose his will on the UO Commander's Council. With all do respect Commander Quita, you berate me on behalf of a Sergeant in order to prove an uncertain point. Have you no respect for my status?"

Commander Quita responds, "It was nothing personal Commander, your ignorance to the obvious threat that has developed left me no choice but to react as such. Even to those whom I have the utmost respect, I will still only exhibit such respect when deserved."

Ziel now raises her voice, "And my actions today proved unworthy of your respect?"

Quita responds, "No, your words and actions over the past few cycles have shown me that."

Commander Blenko jumps in, "Please my fellow officers, let's all just calm down, we can talk this out. I'm sure if we just think rationally a compromise can be reached."

Commander Tilk pushes to the same end, "I agree, we cannot have ill feelings develop amongst the Commanders. To be our most effective, all twenty of us must remain a cohesive unit."

Quita replies defiantly, "There's no room for negotiation. My ruling will remain as it was laid out within the session. I've reviewed dozens of past council sessions where this threat was discussed, and honestly I was sickened by what I saw. The bias and contempt held by many of our commanders towards subordinates is an outrage. And why is this, why would the top officials in an organization such as ours view something with such disdain? Is it because there are not facts to support the claims? Is it because we do not have the means to take action? No, it's because the proper chain of command was not followed and the Council refuses to ever play the part of the fool. Well I'll tell you what's foolish, to ever give Narel any classification other than that of a serious threat. Our field lieutenants, sergeants, and privates are our eyes and ears to what's happening out there. They are Utopera's senses, present within the Verse at all times and pumping information back to us; vital data that needs to be given constant and careful consideration. Please commanders, put pride and ego aside, the actions made have been justified and are past the point of necessity. Even if none of you believe that Narel is a real threat, you must see that the people of the Verse are more than convinced. Therefore if nothing else, panic itself is a looming threat to us. We cannot allow the people to lose faith in the UO, and by ignoring their pleas we will do just that. Mace Crimson may not have achieved the rank of commander just yet, but his actions over the past few years make him more deserving than some; yet still he's been met by as much resistance to his investigation from his superiors as he has from his enemies. That's all I have to say on the matter, I will submit my resignation if my orders are revoked by any means."

Blenko and Tilk both concede and shake arms with Quita before dismissing themselves from the Archives Hall. Ziel on the other hand storms out, disrespecting all three commanders without a single farewell.

Back on the Asteroid, Mace moves off the neutral terrain and into the mysterious jungle. As he breaks through the thick brush he is greeted by flowers and shrubs of all different shapes and colors. Some seem to be conscious as they sway on their own accord or quickly snap at insects that wonder too close. Many different winged insects along with creepy-crawlies litter the vegetation as well as the jungle floor. Small reptiles and primates also scurry about, while the much larger species can be heard sending loud calls across the forest. As Mace moves deeper into the thick foliage, the landscape seems to change. Trees and shrubs become much more stemmy, with long, winding branches and thick, swirling trunks that wrap and twirl around each other as well as the surrounding undergrowth. The maze of shrubs soon form into a fence-like obstacle that Mace is forced to crawl through. In a few places the extensive overgrowth blocks out most outside light; however other areas tend to be slightly more open and can be navigated steadily as long as you have a significant amount of upper body strength and even more endurance. At one point the soldier climbs to the peak of the intertwined branches. The long, stable limbs make for easy foot grips and from his elevated position he looks for a more clear route. The soldier peers out to see a much more open territory up ahead that leads to some sort of enshrinement. He then climbs back down and changes course for the more suitable path. He can't see the main structure in detail, but it's definitely big and definitely artificial.

After another hour of navigating through the dense branches the forest finally opens back up. Mace is again amazed at the sight, in front of him lies a small city of ruins. Large, finely carved stone and clay structures litter the apparently abandoned city, which has now become neglected and overgrown. In the distance, a large pyramid can be seen that sits within a depressed valley, this keeps it from protruding up above the treetops, most likely an effort to hide the city from those who seek it out. The structures were truly breathtaking, Mace hadn't seen such masterful clay and stone architecture since he viewed Earth's historical structures while still a young child. As he walked the city, he examined the various writings and patterns carved or painted onto the surface of every structure. He doesn't understand the words, yet still Mace feels as though he's gathering a picture of the civilization. They don't seem to be all that much different from his own, seeking to find harmony in an unbalanced and chaotic Universe.

As he reaches the pyramid, Mace runs into a dead end. He attempts to walk through the door, but the interior of the pyramid is pitch black and he is faced with a wall less than fifteen feet inside. Figuring that the indigenous people wouldn't build and protect this pyramid without ample reason, Mace creates a makeshift torch and re-enters the megalithic structure. As he inspects the wall which impedes his progress, no simple solution to the obstruction pops out at him. The barrier seems to be solid and immovable, but as Mace takes a quick glance at what lies above him, he becomes curious. The chamber seems to shift and continue upward, ascending higher into the pyramid. With no ladder or foot holes, climbing would seem impossible but Mace is not easily denied. He kicks and digs into the loose rock in the walls and attempts to climb. After making it about six feet up, his right foot displaces a large chunk of rock and he comes crashing back down. As he lies on his back discouraged and frustrated, Mace begins to consider exactly what he's doing. While in the midst of becoming fed up, he glances over to pick up his torch and illuminates an area where he displaced part of the pyramid wall. Behind the rocks sits a crudely carved, metal lever. Mace hops to his feet and pulls the lever, it takes all of his might to budge but the angry soldier will not be denied. Once the lever gives way, a hissing noise can be heard coming from above. As Mace raises his torch back up, a long serpent like object can be seen dropping rapidly from above. Fearing the worst, Mace jumps out of the way and falls back into the hallway. As the serpent hit's the floor Mace lunges towards the guardian, using his torch as a weapon. To his delight however, he lunges at a mere rope, hanging from high within the chamber. Mace had inadvertently stumbled upon the correct entrance. He climbs the rope and is astonished at how high the chamber stretches. Eventually he passes the point at which he felt as though he should have reached the top of the pyramid, and it just continues even farther. He presses on, engravings are carved throughout the entire chamber and although Mace doesn't have the time nor energy to read them all; he's still captivated by some of the symbols and imagery. They are colorful and eloquent, how they were inscribed within this chamber is a mystery, and quite the achievement. His torch goes out, but Mace has come much too far to turn back now. What were these people protecting within this pyramid, and more importantly did they know anything that could help him get out of this place.

He finally reaches the top of the pyramid and at this point the wall in front of him finally gives way. Mace climbs on top of the ledge and as he lets go of the rope he is surrounded only by darkness. He looks back to the rope which is now invisible to him and says aloud, "Getting back down should be fun."

At this point, the blinded soldier cannot see an inch in front of him and he carefully tries to feel his way around the dark corridor. There seems to be nothing but open space around him and the only guide wall he has is on the left. He sticks close to this last point of orientation, attempting to guide himself in any way possible.

Step after step nothing changes until suddenly Mace feels a slight elevation of the surface under his lead foot. He reaches his right leg out and presses down with a small amount of weight to distinguish the unexpected change when the tiny ledge gives way and releases the ground beneath him. It seems that the change he felt was a booby trap, when that area was stepped on the flat ground in front of him dropped and turned into a hard-angled slope. Without his footing, Mace slides out of control down the dark ramp and into the unknown. The slope twists and turns, with the steep incline increasing his speed by the second. As the ramp straightens, Mace is able to at least regain some of his balance and sit up as he slides, his armor scraping and sometimes sparking as he coasts uncontrollably. Suddenly, he begins to feel damp; for some reason the slope is becoming wet and slick. The water makes for a smoother ride but Mace still has no way to stop himself. There is no visible source to the incoming water, but the volume seems to be gradually increasing. Eventually, while hydroplaning faster and faster down the slick slope Mace sees a glimmer of light out in the distance beneath him. It approaches quickly, as it finally nears however the water is practically engulfing him, now freely flowing onto the slope. It tosses him around erratically, causing him to become disoriented. After rounding one more turn Mace is slung around and thrown violently into a raging river. He pops up to the surface and can see light up ahead, but doesn't have long to recover as the furious waters quickly send him over a towering waterfall. As he's tossed about, Mace manages hold his breathe, but fails to close his eyes as he's overwhelmed with the ability to use them once again. He plummets a long way down, crashing into the pool below like a boulder. After the splash clears there is no sign of poor Crimson.

Upon closer examination, the unyielding soldier frantically swims for the surface after submerging a couple dozen feet due to the long fall. He elevates quickly from the depths of the reservoir and breaks the water's plane gasping for air. The extremely fortunate soldier takes deep breathes as he regains himself until gingerly swimming towards solid land. Confused about exactly where he is, Mace inspects the well-carved-out inner chamber of the pyramid, if he's even inside the pyramid anymore. Light seems to come from beneath the reservoir and a blue glow cascades around the artificial cavern. The ceilings are high and finely chiseled, while some sort of dull purple stalactite formations are scattered about indicating leaks from outside. As he gets back to his feet, Mace inspects the chamber more closely. There are numerous open shafts along the outer perimeter of the structure leading deep into the ground. As Mace walks over and peers into one, he can see some faint beams of light dancing off the minerals buried beneath. Surprised by his ability to view the trace amounts of light that make it into the shaft, Mace quickly realizes that these tunnels are mine shafts and most likely that of diamond mines. Looking around at the sheer number of harvest sites, he now understands what this pyramid is protecting. This must be the largest concentration of diamond in the Verse, just one of these mines would produce enough Capital to buy your own system.

He then walks over to a second, much smaller spring located directly in the center of the chamber. This spring was secluded from the first, and looked to be quite shallow. Still, strangely the water glowed noticeably brighter than the other, much larger reservoir. Next to the spring, a large half-wall depicts a vivid illustration of some epic battle. The images look to have been created using engraving tools and some primitive forms of paint. Judging by the erosion and primal means used to create the work, Mace estimates that the drawings are ancient. The conflict looks to be between two powerful enemies, each controlling a formidable military. The first leader was followed by an army of light; soldiers bearing white and green armor followed a warrior that stood tall and shined vibrantly during the battle. The second, much larger creature led an army of darkness, one that fought viciously using any means granted to them in order defeat the enemy. There were apparently four large, colored engravings when the original artist(s) created the work. Four images depicting an incredible tale, one that Mace couldn't help but be drawn into. He began to examine the images further, taking note to the subtleties of the battle.

The dark soldiers, who mostly appeared scarred and disfigured; dressed in strictly black armor and would often be seen striking enemies down from behind or violently murdering those already subdued. The observant soldier also quickly notices that the army of light amasses a fair group of prisoners as the images progress, while the dark army doesn't hold a single one throughout the entire sequence.

He moves down the line until reaching the forth image where not much can be seen, at least not anymore. Here, the surface of the wall has been stripped down or grinded away by something. Only a rough outline of the image and a few shades of color remain in its place.

He focuses back on the viewable engravings. Within each picture, there is at least one area of land supporting battle and one area of ocean or sea. Those images also show some type of aerial conflict as well, with the dark forces being more prevalent throughout the sky. Mace also is given the impression that the dark force likes to attack unexpectedly, as their naval units are often seen submerged beneath the surface or hovering high above it, always seeking a sneak attack. Their assaults on land and through the air also all seem to come either from the flank or via sabotage. White forces are seen sitting atop the sea surface openly, prepared to battle the enemy honorably, face-to-face. It's clear to Mace that the dark army is the invading force. After the first image, which shows the battle begin with both sides commencing attacks at full strength, it looks as though the light forces are easily defeating their dark adversaries. Going into the second battle, the forces of light much outweigh the dark army. It appears victory will grace them sooner rather than later, until some unclear outside factor results in the loss of a large portion of the light army. The image points to a side engraving, one added just above the second image. This side art shows what looks like a star system or planet grouping engulfed in some sort of explosion, but Mace can't make it out for certain. One thing he knows for sure is that whatever this image depicts, is catastrophic. A large blast wave surrounds whatever it once was.

Moving onto the third image, a drastic change is seen. Whatever occurred within the second scene has made the dark ruler much stronger and even his physical size in the drawing has increased. Now much larger than the light ruler, his armies have been reinforced and his prisoners stranded along the other side are freed. Far outnumbering their adversary and claiming significant tactical advantage, the dark armies attack subtly no more. Both forces meet head on and the final battle commences. Mace feels a strange chill as he gazes upon this third image, and he peers over at the forth one more time, insatiably curious about what it once displayed.

He walks away from the ancient wall and back past the small, gleaming spring. As he strolls by, the soldier can read the words, Ver of Vita carved next to the steps of the pool. He looks more closely over the unknown terms until a noise can be heard coming from a dark corner of the chamber. Mace is overcome with the feeling that he needs to investigate and proceeds to the corner carefully. As he walks over the noise can be heard getting louder, it was a swooshing noise as though fabric or cloth was being brushed across rock. As he peers through two megaliths intersecting at the base of the chamber, he finds a small passageway that exists between the rock. The sound is undoubtedly coming from this spot and as he draws nearer it grows louder. As he bends over to inspect, the noise becomes stronger and unrelenting. Mace's hand sits against the stone wall of the chamber when he begins to feel some rapid vibrations. The soldier doesn't get to conjure another thought before twin streams of water come racing down from the ceiling above, filling the temple chamber. He's swept off his feet by the raging tide and forced right through the tiny passageway. The soldier struggles for air as he races down the pyramids' water filled tunnels once more. He's spun around a few more times until he wraps around one final large turn before being spewed out into the jungle. The soldier falls through a tree and down a muddy embankment created by the flood water. He slides into a murky reservoir where he lies motionless for a time, trying yet again to regain his composure.

As the soldier continues gasping for air, bewildered by the fact he's been able to survive the never ending obstacles of this strange day, he sits up to realize that despite his armor one of his ribs has been cracked by that last fall. He attempts to cover the wound and tightens his abdominal armor while gazing up at the pyramid. It would seem as though he's been spit out the back of it, and from here the base of the structure can be seen stretching deep below the jungle floor out front. Mace spots a partially dilapidated mud brick dwelling, located just a few hundred yards away and makes his way over. He removes the few survival supplies still being carried as well as the lone food ration retrieved from his ship. The soldier takes off his armor and fixes up the shelter with a few wide, flat leaves picked and used as a canopy. This, coupled with some fluffy moss found scattered about that works nicely as bedding provides him a decent shelter. The injured and exhausted Crimson seeks some rest, and the stresses he's endured this day warrant such a need. To warn him of any intruders, Mace breaks apart some dry juntha twigs. These branches produce a loud crackling sound when broken that will surely cause him to wake were they to be crushed or stepped upon. He eases back on his makeshift bed and rips open the only food ration he has. The dazed soldier doesn't think about much as he eats, but he does feel a strange sense of calm come over him. Although he faced nothing but turmoil this day, something here allows him to feel at ease, a state that this particular UO soldier had not felt in some time. Soon after the ration hits his stomach Mace is fast asleep, never even realizing he'd closed his eyes.

Aboard the UO Cruiser Irenus, Brutus and his rescue team have finally reached zone 186 and are approaching Mace's last known transponder position. As Brutus gazes out a large observation window within his quarters, he inspects the layout of this somewhat dead location. All that appears to be present is a bunch of rock and other debris orbiting about. He's already researched this asteroid belt through the ship's database console and knows that the belt itself orbit's a black hole, one which currently resides two sectors away. The orbit is stable and unwavering, nothing major is set to intersect with the belt's trajectory for two more years. Mace should have been afforded some fairly smooth travel through this region, with nothing irregular or anomalous to interfere. Brutus reads over a few more notes, then heads down to address his team before beginning the search. As some of the members who partake in this mission were appointed by Commander Ziel, they are predisposed to disagree with Brutus' objective. Word has already been spreading throughout the small fleet that Mace is long dead, and that this whole rescue attempt is a pointless waste of time as well as resources. Brutus on the other hand is convinced that he will find his friend here and the newly appointed UO officer has never felt more confident about any mission.

He reaches the main bridge and walks over to a platform elevated just above and behind the cruiser's pilots. Before getting the chance to give out his first command since arriving, Sergeant Tailkon already has something to say.

He approaches Brutus with an arrogance to his march, "All of our scanners and scopes are negative on finding a location that can even possibly sustain life. If Lieutenant Crimson crashed here, he's surely dead."

Brutus ignores the comment and turns away unconvinced.

Tailkon raises his voice, "If you don't believe me just ask Delaini!"

Corporal Hela Delaini, chief radus analyst for the rescue fleet looks over to Brutus. She seems hesitant to speak, reluctant to be the bearer of bad news, "No signs of life Sergeant, just asteroids and debris as far as the scopes can see. Sensor reception is at full connectivity, there's almost no chance anything could be out there.
The entire zone is negative."

"There", Sergeant Tailkon says, "what more must we discuss?" Brutus walks over to one of the bridge control boards and
flips a switch that activates a ship-wide intercom system. He picks up the microphone and begins to address the fleet. All hands stop what their doing in order to listen up as the operation's leader speaks.

"To every being apart of this mission. I don't know what you've heard about what's happened out here, or the task that's been placed upon us, but I'll tell you how it really is. Lieutenant Crimson's transponder gave its last fleeting transmission somewhere within the coordinates where we sit right now. That's right Mace Crimson, plenty of you know him personally and I'd assume that the majority of you at least know of him. He's not the type of soldier to roll over and die…not ever. If you don't know him, you've probably heard some pretty incredible stories about him; never sure of what to believe because many of them are quite fantastic, even spectacular. I wouldn't believe them myself if boasted by another soldier, but I can tell you from firsthand experience that every tale you've ever heard about him is true."

The ship is silent, as every soldier aboard can sense their commanding officer's sincerity.

"So if there's any possibility that an organism could survive out here…whether it's for five seconds or one millisecond, we're gonna keep looking. Anyone who has a problem with that can come see me personally and will be excused from the mission. You will be sent back to Utopera immediately. Now, all pilots to fighters, transports, and scanning ships. We're beginning a grid by grid search of every asteroid out there, a detailed schematic and zone breakdown has been uploaded to your ships. Stick to your search grid and good luck, there's no time dilation in this galaxy so let's go, the clock on Crimson's life could be ticking!"

Off in Jakaruk or what's more commonly called the Spear Galaxy due to its odd appearance, Narel makes his final approach towards the planet Lustrum. This dark, forest-covered planet is actually a large moon distantly orbiting the gas giant Colypsis. The planet is cold, but it catches enough heat from Colypsis for its thick atmosphere to produce an effective greenhouse effect. Although the moon looks as though it may have been gaseous itself due to thick cloud and fog cover, it's actually a natural, organism-developing planet with varying indigenous species. This lively world is covered with tall, wide-bodied trees stretching high into the skies in order to pick up scant solar rays from neighboring stars, bouncing around between clouds. A thick fog covers the planet at all times, varying in intensity by the minute. Sometimes you may have thirty or forty feet of visibility in front of you for a majority of the day, then suddenly a wave, as the Beluans call a thick patch of fog, moves in and after it reaches you one cannot see six inches in front of them.

Narel's fighter passes by an outer perimeter of Nexcin starships. Six of the mammoth war giants sit along a well-spread, single line formation facing the merky planet. Sitting just above them, appearing to watch over the rest of the fleet formation is the most mammoth starship in the Nexcin fleet and probably the Verse for that matter. It is known as the Malacaus and it's size and capacity are nearly ten times that of an average starship, holding an estimated 4.7 million Nexcin soldiers and crew. The immense superstructure has three tiers or main sections which narrow from back to front, giving it a slight aerodynamic appearance. Two large ejection tubes protrude from the front and back of the craft, they're used to propel troops as well as explosives and supplies deep into enemy controlled territory. The starship is equipped with both warp generators and a balanced anti-matter thruster system allowing the giant vessel to perform intergalactic travel with general ease. This ship is the crowning jewel of Narel's fleet.

He draws ever closer and flips on his com unit to identify himself to fleet command. He contacts the Malacaus directly, "This is Narel, I'll be landing on the surface shortly. Prepare command for my arrival."

The fleet coordinator, a Nexcin lieutenant replies immediately, "Yes my lord, we've been expecting you. The command center is located at coordinates 143-87. Would you like a spotter to take you down, we've lost countless units amidst the fog?"

Narel ignores this last question and simply proceeds on course. He descends upon the moon, his ship looking like a tiny black spec as it drifts above the backdrop of this deep white abyss. If one didn't know that a solid surface existed below, they may honestly confuse this place for a gas or vapor moon. Bands of thick, saturated clouds cover the planet and scatter any image of the surface one would hope to capture. Narel has already loaded the moon's topography and will have to land blind as visibility will remain minimal down to about fifteen feet above ground level.

As his ship breaches the atmosphere, it's immediately lost within the dense cloud cover. The warlord is unaffected by the loss of vision, he calmly closes his eyes as he allows the instruments to guide him down. He plummets through the sea of fog, fully concentrating on his surroundings in a somewhat meditative state while attempting to get a feel for the planet. At the last moment Narel awakens from his trance and manually overrides the controls. He pulls up and changes his landing zone, canceling out the precise coordinates meant to set him down within a Nexcin-controlled docking strip. Instead, the powerful tyrant lands the fighter in an uncharted area and quite masterfully, in fact with little more than a slight jolt as the ship gingerly drops out of the fog.

He quietly steps out of the ship and opens the rear cargo bay. Inside, he unlocks a compartment stocked with an ample supply of weaponry, survival supplies, and survey equipment. The Nexcin Leader grabs only his plasma staff and closes the bay door. He then accesses a hidden keypad just below the rear thruster. The digital screen takes him through various options until Narel enters a code that activates the fighter's unique security system. A liquid metal coating begins to leak from atop the ship and hardens evenly as it progressively flows from section to section. As this metallic coating encases every crevice of the fighter, two drill-like instruments protrude from beneath the ship and begin drilling into the ground. In under a minute, the ship is securely anchored and impenetrably shielded from attack.

With his fighter secured, the warlord turns toward the forest. As he takes his first step, a noise can be heard from not far away. Narel closes his eyes, then opens them sharply as if to stare through the fog. He looks around and around, until suddenly from above, a lupavore jumps from a perch high within one of the towering treetops. These beastly, wolf-like creatures have six razor sharp claws on each of their four paws. They often run quadrupedally, but are more than capable of standing on their hind legs to walk or fight. They are primitive beasts with a below-average intelligence, yet they can be resourceful and extremely ruthless. They're known to slice and attack a target mercilessly, regardless of the enemy's response or level of hostility. They do not possess the vocal abilities to speak the Versal language although some lupavores understand a sizeable portion of common speech. Their race has been enslaved by Lustrum's alpha species, the Beluans. They are trained to fight and attack all enemies who threaten their primitive leaders.

Narel senses the attack coming and knocks the animal aside just as it falls into range, the lupavore rolls over once and flips back onto four feet, regaining it's balance immediately. The beast growls as it digs it's long, sharp claws into the ground, challenging the evil conqueror. Narel stares down the bloodthirsty beast and moves into a battle position, spreading his legs slightly and tilting his staff about forty-five degrees, openly challenging the creature right back. Just as he's about to make his move, another Lupavore ferociously attacks from out of the fog, lunging in and jumping up behind Narel, attempting to clamp it's vice-like jaws down on his neck. The warlord spins around with great force, almost levitating for a moment as the attacking canine is thrown off of him. It slides across the forest floor coming to rest next to it's pack mate, who seems to be enraged by Narel's resilience. The Lupavores regroup and spread out to attack once more, their haggard claws clenching with angst. The two growl ferociously and circle the warlord. He drops back into his stance, pretending like he's going to engage both the beasts, but Narel is not one to be fooled twice. As his rabid adversaries grind their claws on the mud and rock below their feet, Narel fakes like he's about to lunge before abruptly turning his plasma staff sideways and crouching slightly. Flying through the fog are two more, little-suspecting lupavores who planned to finish the attack their two brothers started. They converge on Narel at full speed, never seeing him open his weapon through the dense fog. Both the lupavores are impaled, one through the chest and the other through it's neck. Narel then rips the plasma staff out through the top of their carcasses, which drop to the ground mutilated. As he twirls his staff around relieving it of a thick coat of blood, the two remaining beasts turn tail and run with blazing speed through the fog.

Narel smirks as they evade him, but he's not the type to just let something get away after an attempt on his life. The warlord hunts the beasts through the fog, following their every move, displaying blazing speed of his own. The Lupavores begin to yelp as they now run solely on adrenaline and intense fear, both instinctively knowing that bi-pedal beings cannot normally keep up with them.

As their speed increases and the two maneuver through some thick brush they soon lose sight of Narel. They continue to run at full steam until they reach an old Nexcin base that had been overtaken by the Beluans for a time and since abandoned. As the two beasts race through the empty base they have to pass through a narrow enclosure between an old armory and vehicle depot. They approach the tunnel-like enclosure coming together side by side right as the pair nears the end. Suddenly, the beasts see two lights appear through the fog, looking similar to the plasma chambers they saw cut up their pack mates. It is to late for them to stop now, and before they even fully realize what their running into, Narel's plasma staff brings them to a screeching halt. The warlord provides immovable resistance and these lupavores are mutilated even worse than their fallen pack mates, both practically cut in half. He killed all four without even swinging his weapon.

Narel stands up and looks around the overrun Nexcin base, embarrassed by it's concession to these primitive beasts. He peers over the dismembered and partially consumed remains of hundreds of Nexcins, his rage growing with each thought that passes through his vast and radical mind. Rage towards Lustrum, rage towards the Beluans, and the most anger seems to be towards his own forces. He feels disgraced by what he's witnessing.

The warlord turns back to the thick forest just as a brief break in the fog surrounds him. The forest is much larger and plant infested than one can infer, as many trees and vines stretch for hundreds if not thousands of feet into the air. They cross and intersect, climbing one another in a desperate attempt to reach for sparse cosmic rays. Also, massive fungi and mosses cover everything, stretching themselves across the lands equally. Some tree bases look to have a diameter nearly ten times the size of Narel's fighter, at least a few hundred feet in circumference..

The fog is quick to roll back in, yet Narel continues to look around, as if unhindered by the lack of visibility. He makes no attempt to stay within the eye of the cloud cover and instead continues to move into the thicker bands of fog until he reaches an area where nothing can be seen at all. He then continues on his original path back towards the Nexcin encampment.

Aboard Brutus' Cruiser, he's somehow managed to doze off while awaiting the results of his search and recon efforts. The stress and exertion of will must have taken it's toll on him. Inside this sleep Brutus' mind drifts far away…

He sees Mace standing atop a mountain, surrounded by the most incredible paradise one can imagine. Brutus descends from the clouds, gradually moving towards his friend. The wind is fierce and it's difficult to make it down, but Brutus knows that they can make it. Mace is looking for help, and it appears he's been hurt pretty bad. As he moves in to save his friend, the seconds begin to feel like hours and every inch they move crawls by slower, until suddenly it fades away altogether. Before he can make it down to Mace, Brutus wakes up. As soon as his eyes hit the fresh air he is wide awake, noticing that he passed out while sitting up his chair. The dream was so vivid, he felt as

though Mace had been right in front of him. The dream shook the already emotional soldier as he cleaned himself up to await his team's data. After washing his hands and face, Brutus cannot shake the ominous dream and he takes a hot shower in an attempt to regain his focus and concentration. The worried soldier knows that Mace has escaped many dire situations in the past, but for his beacon to simply
disappear, something told Brutus that this time he really needed help.

Back on Lustrum, Narel strolls into the Nexcin camp as if he were walking down his own private drive. His outline appears first through the fog, startling many of his soldiers who think he's a Beluan, assumingly scouting out an impending attack. They open their staffs to which Narel instantly shouts out, "Close your weapons or I'll make you wish I was one of these pathetic creatures."

The Nexcins quickly recognize the voice of their leader and follow his command. They open the gate to the base and allow him to pass without another word. He walks through the gates, the remaining perimeter of the base is protected by a powerful electromagnetic fence. If an individual walks between any two fence posts an electromagnetic wave is released. The discharge will pin any metal object within the field using a powerful magnetic stream while a devastating electric shock is sent through the intruder. The fence surrounding this base has several layers of additional posts added to accommodate the Beluans. These mammoth creatures rarely ever wear armor which makes the magnetic field fairly useless, they are also strong enough to push through a single wave of electricity, even on maximum power. With multiple waves of the pylons set up, the electrical discharge is too much for even the largest Beluan to handle.

As Narel moves through the base, each Nexcin he passes bows to their leader. The warlord doesn't even acknowledge them, he simply continues on unescorted, seeking out his officers. He eventually encounters a group of them, apparently preparing a search party.

Narel interrupts, speaking to the soldier leading the briefing, "Captain Varik, are you in charge of this facility?"

"Yes my lord", He replies, "Since Commander Gruk was dismembered almost five cycles back. We were just sending out a search party to locate you."

Narel glares down at the Nexcin with a disturbing expression, "Do I look like I need a search party Captain?"

The Nexcin remains silent.

"I simply decided that I should see first hand what type of superior combat force could possibly impede my battalions in such a way. I thought to myself, the beasts of Lustrum must truly be a spectacle for the ages in order to halt my lines. Yet, to my surprise, I arrive to find a lowly batch of inferior life, without even the technology to build their own bases."

The Nexcin ruler pauses for a moment before raising his voice, "I provide you with reinforcements, infinite supplies, and ample time, yet these beasts still defy you! I want an explanation Captain."

"In my defense", the Nexcin cautiously replies, "the enemy is extremely knowledgeable of their home planet and they use ambush tactics that make our technological advantage useless. Their size coupled with the fog makes it impossible to attack from a distance and they become a much larger threat when attacking from just inches away. Their savage nature also allows the lupavores and underling Beluans to battle without the fear of death, making their actions unpredictable. We're starting to make progress, now that we've decided to pick and choose our battles, even retreating if necessary. This strategy has led us to the recovery of four critical territories over the last three cycles."

Narel continues to look over the Captain with distain, "This planet should have been entirely overtaken in less than three cycles. Your time to complete this mission is up, I'll take care of it now. Show me where the Beluan leader is most likely to be."

A nearby lieutenant pulls out an E-pad and brings up a map of the area. He hands the E-pad to Captain Varik who begins to outline a path. Narel looks over his soldier as he continues and scowls, "This seems to be a very indirect route Captain, do I seem interested in the sites to you?"

Varik replies, "No, my lord its just that many of the roads leading to their main stronghold are under Beluan control and therefore impassable."

Narel's expression manages to leak further disgust as he now becomes irate. Without another word the Nexcin ruler pulls out his plasma staff and stabs Captain Varik through the side of his armor, never even opening the chambers. He pushes so hard that the metal point of his staff goes clear though Varik's body on a sharp upward angle and out the other side, pressing against the opposite shoulder plate of the Captain's armor. Narel then twists and pulls the staff out, leaving Varik's body to fall to the floor, dead before he hit's the ground. Some of the Nexcin officers are surprised by this and even angered, but none make a single move in fear that their intentions could be mistaken and they would be next.

Narel stands there silent for a moment before saying, "weakness is like a cancer, and I won't have it spread throughout my ranks. We attack, we destroy, we conquer; no compromise, no surrender, and no prisoners that is the Nexcin way. Now can one of you draw me a DIRECT route to the enemy leader?"

The Lieutenant, Bril Razu, pulls the e-pad from Varik's dead hands and erases what's been outlined. He then quickly draws an undeviating course to the Beluan stronghold. Narel says to Razu, "thank you Captain."

Over on the mysterious asteroid, Mace awakens just as a star seems to rise in the northeast. Mace still does not at all understand the seemingly impossible characteristics of this strange place; drastically different climates all located within a shared ecosystem, numerous odd species which he cannot identify, and a star that seems to rise even though Mace remembers no local star shining before his crash. As he stares at the odd horizon, the befuddled soldier cannot see the clouds that seemed to encircle the asteroid when he approached it the day before. Instead now he only sees clear skies and what appears to be a very stable atmosphere. Now rested, Mace pulls himself up off the ground and begins to scout the area for the best path to take. The soldier sheds his armor for a bit and climbs a tall, weeping tree with cascading red leaves. He can see clearly for quite a distance from the top and after his encounters with the changing landscape one day prior he now decides to head across the largest solid plateau he can see and from there move up onto a lone mountain, sitting off by itself, far into the distance. Mace doesn't know why, but he is drawn to this spot and believes that this is likely the location of the unknown entity he's now twice encountered. Mace takes a deep breathe of the crisp morning air and can't help but admire the beauty of this ominous place before heading towards more steady terrain. Despite the trials and injuries he faced the day before, the veteran soldier felt surprisingly better this morning. Even his rib which was clearly cracked yesterday, was now barely even noticeable, just a little tender to the touch. It was quite curious, but also quite pleasing as he was clearly going to need his health and strength if he's going to get out of this place.

It's not long before his new path takes Mace out of the thick foliage and into some new territory. The revitalized soldier makes quick work of a flat patch of land covered with large, thorn covered bushes. Some of the thorns are nearly a foot long and sharp enough to sever flesh. Small, aggressive, short-winged creatures swing from between the thorns, and they seem to be eating some sort of nectar found in pods located at the base of certain thorn patches. Mace is unsure of what this species is but he's fascinated by them. They also hang onto and jump through the patch using their long, whip-like tongues to disable and catch food, usually small creatures and insects. Their stubby little wings aid them in swinging between the thorns, but appear unable to produce sustained flight.

After Mace maneuvers through this dangerous brush he reaches a tropical canyon that looks to extend deep into the core of the asteroid. Looking down into the subterranean paths which spiral deep beneath the ground, it can be seen that these under levels are teeming with life that seems to grow richer the deeper he gazes. Were he to have fallen in, Mace would be faced with a whole new world to escape, that's if he could even survive the fall. This hidden death trap couldn't even be seen from Mace's vantage point earlier this morning and it's an obstacle that isn't easy to overlook or overcome. Ferns and large-leafed tropical plants of all colors dominate the landscape and solid ground can rarely be seen when peering into the cavernous depths below. Mace can see some very large animal trails within the trees and numerous gas vents where vapor is likely released from the distant ground. The ever crafty Mace scours the landscape around him for anything that can be used to avoid this treacherous obstruction. There is no safe way to enter the canyon, the walls seem to go vertical for at least eighty feet in the most shallow regions. Even if he were to get down, getting back out would be impossible.

Staring through this unavoidable challenge, an idea comes to him shortly; it's not exactly ingenious but hopefully it'll do the job. He gathers a pair of large stems from a batch of fern plants surrounding him, then, using them as an anchor he attempts to cross the canyon by scaling the outer rim, thus staying atop the deep ravine and never actually being forced to enter. It is a difficult trek even for Mace, as the humidity rising from the canyon makes him sweat profusely; this in turn drenches the fern stems he clings to and makes it quite challenging to maintain a solid grip. He uses the stems to keep his balance, poking them through the ground until he can find a stable foothold. The outer rim of the canyon has an unstable edge of intertwined brush completely tangled in knots, very loose in some spots but tightly knit in others. Mace inches ever so slowly through the brush, careful not to shift his weight all at once. He slips several times, but much to the disappointment of a local group of scavengers who've congregated below in hopes of an easy meal, the young Lieutenant makes it across safely. Once past the canyon Mace feels great both mentally and physically; his strength and endurance seem to have caught a second wind and he wants to keep his adrenaline flowing. Momentum is a soldiers greatest ally, but he's never felt a rush like this before. All that stood between him and the plateau he seeks is an ice covered plain that extended right into the plateau wall. This open area creates a funneled path for airflow, producing substantial crosswinds. Mace wastes no time, he takes his undershirt off and tightens it around his head in order to help protect from wind burn. He then secures his armor and starts a mad sprint across the windy field focused on one thing, reaching that mountaintop.

He pushes through the sheering winds with pure determination and eventually reaches the plateau, surprisingly enough he 's barely out of breathe. It had been at least a mile long sprint across ice-covered land and the exhilarated soldier wasn't the slightest bit fatigued. After a few moments of reflection he continues, quickly attacking the steep rock face and beginning to climb up. Once reaching the top of this cliff, he'll follow the easier terrain atop the plateau for as long as he can. As the soldier jumps and climbs, he's astounded at the ease in which he continues to move. Every time he pulls himself up, his body seems to feel lighter and eventually he feels almost weightless. The soldier pushes this feeling as much as he can while climbing and scampers up a several hundred foot cliff in less than a minute. Once he is within about fifteen feet from the cliff top, Mace gives one final push and leaps to the flat surface above. He looks back at the jagged cliff and rethinks the other two obstacles he has encountered this day still in shock of what's transpired. He feels as though his body has infinite energy and the more he expends the stronger he feels. The soldier stares ahead for a moment and says aloud, almost as if he were talking to the asteroid beneath him, "What is this?"

Back on Lustrum, Narel reaches the ramshackle Beluan stronghold. It consists of a one-level, shapeless, broken down structure with several open access points that could easily be exploited.

Narel wipes a thick coat of Beluan blood from the ends of his staff once again and approaches the main entrance of the base. The gates themselves are missing, but several Beluan soldiers along with their Lupavores stand guard in its place. Narel approaches them slowly, but once the Beluan patrols notice him they release the Lupavores and begin to shout aggressively in their native language.

Five lupavores charge Narel, but they are no match for him. As before, they thrash and claw ferociously, attempting to goad the warlord into over commitment. Aggressively engaging these tamed beasts would undoubtedly leave him wide open to attack from the rest of the pack. The cunning warrior has now completely broken down their simplistic tactics and formulated a strategy that's most effective. This time, he only attacks their limbs, forcefully swinging his staff with speed and finesse. The custom assault is as merciless as it is relentless. He slices at paws and legs while the beasts remain oblivious, still focused on their own over-ambitious attack plan. Most of the pack doesn't even attempt to defend themselves or even run away, although they aren't given much time to decide. They attempt to hop back on their hind legs or snap blindly at Narel in desperation. The ruthless warrior cuts them up quickly, never allowing the savage creatures to even touch him. After just a few swings there are Lupavore appendages all over the ground. He leaves two of their limbless bodies alive as they yelp and cry while rolling helplessly across the rocky path. The powerful warlord then walks up to the Beluans who stand tall in anger and appear to move into a fighting stance.

Narel stares them down, "I need to speak with your leader."

The Beluans glance at each other briefly before turning their attention back to Narel, without a word they then step aside showing their concession. One of them points to a long hallway that leads into the dilapidated base. Narel passes by the three guards without incident, paying them no additional mind and enters the dimly lit hall. As he walks it can be seen that most of the walls within the base have been partially knocked down or destroyed, and almost all the rooms are now at least somewhat interconnected. Nexcin bodies and armor lay scattered throughout the base and some suits are hung as trophies along walls and in corners. Narel searches every room, but only sees soldiers, no sign of their leader. Of the numerous Beluans he encounters inside the base, none choose to attack him. He continues further until the far end of the hall is reached, here he faces a large, solid metal door which is slightly cracked open.

Narel approaches the final room and rips open the large door as if it were made of foil. The door slams against the wall and Narel takes one step through it. Inside, he observes seven particularly large Beluans, each wearing a presentable armor suit. These must be the officers, Narel is surprised that such a primitive species has even established rank.

Six of the juggernauts sit around the largest of them all, a fourteen-foot-tall Beluan who appears to be the Leader of their sect. The giant sits overtop of a half devoured Nexcin corpse; blood, flesh, and drool leak from his open mouth and cover his barbaric face.

Narel walks right up to the corpse and singles out the leader. He stares into the eyes of the Beluan, "Can I assume you speak the Versal language or do I need to use yours?"

"I speak your tongue visitor", The Beluan responds, "but words are the least of your problems. I take it you saw your friends on the way in."

Several of the Beluan soldiers let out loud, obnoxious, grunt-like laughter. "You're actually just in time, we're almost out of food!"

The other Beluans in the room all begin to circle Narel who confidently stands alone. He sighs, showing that he is neither impressed nor worried and bows his head for a moment. The Beluan officers surrounding him inch ever closer until Narel casts out both his arms and a burst of telekinetic energy sends the Beluans behind him flying into the air and through the weak walls of the dilapidated base. The evil warlord turns to one of the now injured Beluan officers, with his arm still raised and with a slight turn of his hand Narel crushes the beasts spine, killing him instantly.

He then says adamently, "If I need to kill every one of you primitive creatures I will, either way I need this planet."

The Beluan leader replies, "There are an infinite amount of my brothers filling this world, you'll need a lot more of your magic to destroy us all."

The Beluan Leader's words inspire a few more of his followers to attack and three of them simultaneously charge Narel. The dark soldier whips out his plasma staff and allows the beasts to close in. The trio reaches him at about the same time and Narel quickly dodges their attacks, watching them over-swing brutishly. He makes the oversized Beluans look sluggish and uncoordinated while cutting them each in several places with the tip of his staff. The task looks easy to Narel, almost like a child teasing a pet. As they clench in pain, Narel stands several feet in front of his wounded and weakened enemies before making a devastating slice with his staff that beheads all three soldiers.

Narel gives a sadistic smile and then with great speed he lunges across the room and knocks the Beluan leader to the ground. The warlord now stands behind him with his arm wrapped tightly around the Beluan's mammoth neck. He overpowers the beast who is nearly twice his size, and dozens of other Beluans now crowd into the room and growl at him. Their groans are empty however, as every one of them stands paralyzed with fear. Never before have they seen their leader incapacitated like this.

Narel leans in close to the ear of his foe, "I do not need my so called magic."

The Beluan struggles for freedom, but Narel only clenches down harder and leans ever closer, "If you continue to oppose me I will stay on this planet and kill every one of you myself, even if it takes a century to do so. If this hasn't convinced you, maybe the hundreds of your friends I left along my walk here will. Now my soldiers are going to set up some necessary outposts immediately. As long as you don't interfere with them any further you will still be free to live on this planet; if you make me come back again you'll lose that privilege. Do you understand?"

The Beluan leader gasps for air and replies, "I understand my lord."

Narel releases the Beluan and raises his hand as though he were going to use his telekinesis again, but the crowd of Beluans behind him quickly scrambles out of the way, wisely giving in to his dominance.

The Warlord smiles, "Ah, so you can learn. Maybe you're not as incompetent as many think."

Narel then strolls out of the Beluan base just as calmly as he walked in and the Beluan Army immediately halts all planned assaults against the Nexcins. True to the Beluan leader's word, he immediately sends out messengers to all his people in a desperate hope to avoid Narel's promised wrath. Word spreads quickly through the Beluan colony and now they will simply move aside when a Nexcin convoy passes through or sets up shop.

As he walks out into the Lustrum forests, the accomplished warlord pulls a small communicator with video link from a compartment within his armor. He calls over to the Captain, who anxiously awaits word from his leader.

"Yes lord Narel", says Captain Razu.

"The Beluans will no longer exhibit resistance to our occupation here. Keep the majority of your ground forces in position for now, in order to insure the transition, within the next few cycles begin sending reinforcements back to the main fleet. If the Beluans go back on their word and attack so much as a single unit within these woods I will need to be notified immediately and directly."

The Captain shakes his head as Narel speaks, wisely never interrupting or asking questions.

The warlord continues, "I'll also be taking the Malacaus with me, it is of no use here any longer. I'll be docking my fighter up there shortly, tell the crew to prepare for our voyage and let the admiral know that I'll be boarding and assuming command. Move him over to the Bladine, it's the next most capable lead starship".

The Captain waits until he is sure Narel has finished listing his commands, then replies, "There is a problem my lord, the Malacaus was damaged by the Beluans during a supply drop just last cycle. Several thrusters and long range systems were damaged. The situation isn't that serious, but the components needed are rare, they can only be purchased and applied within a system that has advanced repair crews and a diverse selection of parts."

Narel is aggravated that his soldiers would even allow a ship as powerful and capable as the Malacaus to be damaged. "How could these primitive creatures even mount an effective attack on such a starship? I fail to see it."

The Captain begins to hastily explain, "Well my lord, a subordinate was in command and the fog...."

He is cut off by Narel, "It's of no matter, I'll take the ship for restoration myself. Prospina isn't too far and we should be able to avoid detection. Have our nav teams map out an obscure flight plan, I don't wish to be spotted. After the repairs are complete I'll take the ship back to the main fleet. Along with my other commands get in touch with our contacts on Prospina, they'll need to know I'm coming."

The Captain responds, "Yes my lord, I'll pass your orders on immediately."

Narel closes the video link and begins the trek back to his fighter.

Brutus' fleet on the other hand still relentlessly continues their search with nothing to show. They've scoured this sector for hours now without finding the faintest sign of Mace or his ship.

Sergeant Weskin, a Terrinean UO officer leads the fighter group within Brutus' fleet and reports in, "Sergeant, we've finished our third sweep of the sector with the an identical result. All grids are negative for life or life-bearing conditions for that matter, there's no way there's someone alive out here. We tried sir and have given it ample time, but I suggest we call off the search."

Brutus becomes annoyed with his fellow Sergeant, but keeps his composure. "Mace Crimson has not been confirmed dead which for all intensive purposes means he is alive, and this was his last known location. As far as this mission is concerned we're not leaving until he's with us, do you understand me Sergeant?"

Sergeant Weskin replies, "You're commanding officer of this mission, so yes Sir. Commencing fourth sweep of the area."

Brutus heads back to his quarters frustrated. He's certain that his friend is alive and out here somewhere, but where? The sector is just so empty, how could the one living organism within this lifeless zone be so incredibly difficult to find. He prints out diagrams of every cluster and body of mass within the sector. The determined soldier then meticulously researches each one and begins compiling a database. He wants to see if the results for any scanner readings have changed over time. On top of that he searches for any anomaly or variance they might have missed with the initial sweeps. Brutus won't give up on his friend, and the thought that this won't end happily doesn't really even cross his mind. He has more faith in Mace than he would have in Tagithus Hashin himself.

He obsessively combs through the images and data, searching for any inconsistency or alteration when a familiar voice greets the Sergeant, "Nice speech, sounded like a Crimson pep talk if I've ever heard one."

Brutus looks up from his work to see Arilla standing before him, as brazen a smile as ever.

"He would be proud of you", she continues, "and you're going to find him, I know it."

"Thanks for the reassurance", Brutus says, "but what makes you so sure?"

"A feeling I get", she says as she looks through some of the material Brutus is now obsessing over. "The same feeling I get whenever we're in some serious danger and Mace looks us in the eye proclaiming, "we'll make it." I felt it as soon as I got here, even without him to save the day for some reason I know it'll be alright."

She pauses and the room goes silent.

"I didn't wanna reveal myself because you seem more focused than I've ever seen...and well I figured there might be a reason you didn't invite me along to help. Besides after the first ten minutes aboard this ship I noticed that you might need some ears below deck if ya get what I mean."

"Yea" says Brutus, "I know exactly what you mean. If this wasn't a UO ship I'd be worried about a mutiny."

Arilla smiles, "Well you don't have to worry about that, but you should be concerned about any other possible way to kill this mission. I can tell you for a fact that at least a hand full of troops on this boat are trying to find cause for ending this search by any means necessary. So keep the crew and your plan in order."

Brutus thinks for a moment, "I appreciate the sentiment really, but don't worry about my plan or the crew, they're the least of my worries. They may be willing to use any means necessary to end this mission, but they have no idea the means I'd use to see it through. I wont leave this sector without Mace aboard the Irenus and since I'm commanding officer I've no doubt that that'll hold true. One thing you can do for me is run a back door sweep of the sector. Follow each wave of scanning crews in a recovery ship and try to pick up any reflected signals they might not have stuck around to receive. How did you happen to accompany this mission anyway?"

"When I heard about Mace I got Major Parra to make a last second addition to the crew. I'll run that sweep now, just know I'll be around if you need anything and I got your back."

As she exits Brutus looks up one more time and says, "Thanks Arilla".

Over on Mace's lost Asteroid he continues to cross this seemingly endless gray plateau. He marches over towering hilltops and across numerous valleys, each brimming with more ever-changing wildlife and plant growth than the last. Much of these species are unrecognizable to even a well-traveled soldier such as himself. Oddly enough, in contrast to the creatures he saw occupying the bottomless canyon earlier, these animals seemed to be much more peaceful and well-balanced. The atmosphere in these parts is much more timid, as compared to the canyon where Mace felt hostility and tension coming his way just from overlooking the ecosystem.

Large insects and small mammals scurry all over the place in these parts, but they don't present any problem to Mace. Each seems to go about it's business, almost seeming oblivious to his presence. He continues to hike until reaching a tropical paradise where a free-flowing river drops off the mountain into a spectacular waterfall and comes to an end within the oasis laid out before him. It drains into a large, diamond-clear lake. The water sparkling in the daylight is a sight of true delight to Mace, as he is in dire need of a drink. He runs towards the heavenly water and as he passes through a small valley filled with large-flowered trees and berry-filled bushes he is again amazed by the magnificence of this place. Once the soldier arrives at the water's edge he sheds his armor and jumps in. The cool lake refreshes him and Mace can't help but be filled with euphoria. For a moment, he thinks of all his stresses, about how much this unforeseen detour has delayed him from his true priorities. Typically these thoughts would bombard him and build up in his mind like magma in a volcano, until he was just about to blow. The thought quickly fades however, as he gets re-immersed within the beauty of the landscape surrounding him, lying back and admiring all the exotic plant life. He notices that the branches are not only covered with flowers but littered with fruit as well; appearing in a variety of sizes, shapes, and colors.

Mace finishes his swim then hops out to taste some of these rare gifts of nature. Before he's done the hungry soldier is sure to sample every fruit the coast has to offer and enjoys each one more than the last. He then lies next to the lakeside and stares up at the mountain he soon plans to conquer, for the first time since he awoke this morning Mace decides to rest, at least until his food settles.

When he finally brings his eyes back down from the mountaintop, which for some reason he can't seem to stop watching, Mace begins to move his finger around the top of the water. He sees the water turn and swirl as water always does, but as he observes his finger in motion something seems different. Mace stares hard, focusing in on the lake, the water volume itself in particular. Although he could see straight down to the lake bottom, Mace concentrates solely on the liquid itself. As he watches, what at first look like tiny organisms can be seen swimming around below the lake surface. As he continues to move his fingers through the water, any of the miniscule organisms his fingertips encounter seem to follow them, yet as soon as Mace notices this they suddenly repel away. The frightened soldier quickly pulls his hand from the water and as he clears the plane of the water's surface, the tiny organisms seem to disappear.

Mace backs away from the lake, almost tripping over some uneven ground before puzzling over the strange anomaly, what could cause such a reaction? Suddenly feeling uneasy, he looks around with an increased awareness, an eerie silence has fallen over the lakeside. The soldier can't help but feel a oneness with the environment, almost as though it was sharing his emotions and feelings. His curiosity now takes over and he again approaches the water's edge, this time looking more broadly, trying to focus on the entire volume of the lake itself. He concentrates hard, visualizing the entire mass with a purely open mind. At first he doesn't see much, but gradually billions of the tiny organisms come into focus. They can be seen crowding the lake, moving with supreme synchronization and taking up every possible space. It now almost looked as though there wasn't any water at all.

He watches them move and shuffle with an oddly familiar harmony, something that told him this was the normal or typical motion of these creatures. Mace bent down to the water's edge once again and returned his fingers to the surface. Realizing his action before must have somehow influenced the tiny critters, the soldier attempts to slow down all of the little swimmers directly surrounding his hand. He closes his eyes.

As his focus deepens, young Crimson can almost feel his senses broaden. The oneness he feels with nature reaches it's maximum intensity and the tiny objects begin to slow down. As their momentum progressively stalls, Mace feels the water's temperature begin to drop. Even with his eyes closed, he feels as though he can still see the water surrounding his fingers, perhaps even more clearly. The organisms begin to decelerate rapidly, until soon they come to a complete stop. It happens so quickly that Mace doesn't even realize his hand has now become frozen into the lake. He tries to pull his arm free, but the piece of ice has grown very large and doesn't want to budge. The chunk of ice engulfing his hand is over four feet in diameter and looks to extend fairly deep below the surface as well. The soldier panics for a moment, nearly rupturing the tendons in his shoulder and elbow from pulling with such ferocity.

Realizing that brute strength is of no help, Mace calms himself down and tries to think of a smarter approach. Inferring that the predicament must have been caused by his own actions, he decides to try attempting to reverse the process. The soldier focuses on the ice and identifies his mysterious little friends yet again, all of which now look to be either barely moving or frozen into place entirely. Mace tries to speed them up, but has a lot of trouble getting them to budge from their solidified positions. They eventually do begin to move again, quite slowly at first as they break free from the stalemate. He focuses hard and constant until enough of the organisms regain motion so that his hand can move and slide within the ice block. After a bit more time and relentless attention, he wiggles and pulls his hand free from the chunk of ice. The large block teeters slightly in the water as the soldier's limb is liberated, an almost circular hole is left behind marking the spot. Mace steps back from the lake once again, his hand shivering and shriveled. He goes over what's just happened in his mind and realizes that these aren't some odd organisms that he's communicating with, it's actually the molecules of the water itself which he is manipulating.

He says with a curious smile, almost questioning himself. "I can see the particles themselves?"

Baffled, he sits beside the lake once more and allows his arm to dry before continuing onward to the mountain.

Glancing up at the horizon of the peculiar asteroid, he says to himself in awe, "What is this place?".

It's a good thing Mace takes this look because off in the distance he sees a violent storm system forming and realizes he'd better finish resting and get on his way again quickly.

Back on Utopera, Major Parra and Lieutenant Lang appraise and discuss the current situation.

Major Parra tells him, "We still have no word from Brutus' fleet and Gilrak's group is already planning on abandoning their search of the first site. The truth of the matter is, if Crimson were still alive out there, our scanners would have spotted him by now. The Commanders have likely already given up."

Lang tries to be optimistic, "Well, Commander Quita didn't put a timetable on the mission and with Brutus in command that cruiser won't be back until they run outta fuel."

"Still", the major replies, "do you think they could actually find him. I mean I have more faith in Mace than any other being I know, but what if he's truly been lost. I've never seen someone reemerge from a sector with no signs of life whatsoever."

Lang sighs, "If Mace is lost then I fear so will be the UO, for at this point he's the only one who can save us."

"We can't think like that" says the Major, "If he is gone we'll have to press on somehow. Even if it's for no other reason than the fact that Mace wouldn't give in."

Aboard the Malacaus, Narel has already arrived within Prospina's orbit and docks up for repairs at one of the numerous low-orbit docking stations surrounding the planet. He hurries off the massive starship as it is the one vessel within his fleet that will draw significant suspicion from civilians within the docking bay. Several of his agents greet him as the Warlord arrives and they quickly ferry him away from the ship to hide on the planet below. The fairly crowded repair port is packed with beings of all races. Narel's agents seem to be mostly Julian, likely ex-soldiers and three of the brawny mercenaries escort the Warlord to a shuttle. As Narel walks, he re-wraps his cloak to cover his face and all exposed skin to conceal his identity as they move.

Narel eventually says, "I need the ship repaired within a matter of hours."

His agent replies, "It's a very large and complicated ship my lord, we'd have to fly in crews from the other docking stations to complete such a task and that could cost...."

Narel cuts him off, "Funds are of no issue you fool, get as many crews as you need I'd like to be off this planet now if I could. Work on the thrusters and interstellar propulsion modules first, we need to leave this system with as minor a trail as such a ship can leave. I will be traveling to the surface alone, if you're needed
again I'll find you."

"Understood", the agent responds, "your shuttle will take you straight down to a private suite, nothing has changed since your last stay."

Narel walks onto his shuttle and closes the door. The rounded off, pentagon shaped shuttle pod is released from the docking station and begins its descent down towards Prospina's surface. As Narel's agents disperse back into the general docking station population, two undercover UO soldiers wearing civilian armor expose themselves from the crowd.

Private Tethera Gaaron looks to her partner Heila Uren, "There's no doubt that was him, contact Utopera."

Uren opens a portable video link with a text caption of "Narel identified" and awaits a signal. Once contact with the UO is made, he is patched straight through to Commander Lozika. Lozika is the active Commander stationed within Utopera's Command Center, known to UO soldiers and the inhabitants of the UO homeworld as "the bow". The bow is the most well-protected point on the planet and from there the entire UO army can be controlled. This carefully guarded center of high command houses a minimum of fifteen high-ranking officers at all times and has the most sophisticated UO equipment and defenses available at any given moment. Every Commander within the UO rotates on a shift schedule to command the bow. While in command, they have the authority to make any decision unchallenged and the orders must be followed or carried out by any and all instructed personnel.

The Commander rushes over to the video link and says, "Private, let me be sure I'm hearing you correctly, am I to understand that you have a positive identification of Narel himself?

Private Uren responds, "Yes sir, my partner and I are both certain. We believe he arrived aboard a massive starship that is in need of serious repairs, he's likely stuck here Commander. His starship is located at repair station 28D, he discretely departed for the planet while the work takes place."

"Great work soldiers", Lozika eagerly replies keep surveillance on the ship and close down all contact with us to avoid that starship catching wind of any transmissions. We'll dispatch the nearest fleet and surround that docking station as soon as they reach your location, for once Narel will be in for a surprise. The fleet will contact you once it's in attack position."

"Yes sir", Uren replies.

Commander Lozika closes the video link and tells his Lieutenant to determine which fleet is in closest proximity to Prospina.

The analysts begins to search the extensive UO deployment grid and Lieutenant Balla identifies the five closest patrols.

"Commander Pollah's fleet is less than two sectors from the target." The lieutenant exclaims.

Commander Oru Pollah, perhaps the best fleet commander presently active within the UO is in control of a five starship fleet not far from Prospina. In the age of long-range space travel, two sectors is practically within spitting distance. He was stationed above the planet Kalor, overseeing the signing of a mining agreement between two refugee colonies who've been fighting over rights to the ore-enriched planet and it's satellites for nearly a decade.

Commander Lozika brings up Pollah on a video link within a matter of seconds and explains the situation objectively, allowing Commander Pollah to decide for himself whether or not he would like to proceed.

Pollah considers the situation carefully and shortly thereafter he replies, "We may never get another chance like this, he's like a ghost anymore. My ships are in prime condition, my crew is rested, and we're fully armed. I'll get him or end him."

"Good to hear." Commander Lozika replies, "I agree entirely but didn't want to push this on you. I'm assembling a Council session, we'll anxiously await the results of your mission. Good luck Commander."

His starships call in the thousands of fighters they have dispersed throughout the Kalor system. Commander Pollah alerts the rest of his forces of the new itinerary and plots a course to Prospina. His starships gather as many of the fleet's fighters as possible, all those who are within close enough vicinity return before the fleet's departure. Those who miss the fleet will have to stay behind, this mission is far too time sensitive for stragglers. In the last minutes before the fleet blasts off, hundreds of UO ships line up outside the long rows and columns of stacked docking bays, returning to standby positions until their new destination is reached. By this time they've heard of the new mission, and every UO soldier within the fleet wants to be a apart of the crew that finally takes down Narel.

About eighty percent of the fleet's ninety-five thousand fighters return back in time to join the mission and moral of the army is high upon departure. While typically quiet and reserved before an operation, the UO teams on these starships are vocal and intense about seizing this opportunity. The fleet looks as prepared and focused as they can be, and with Commander Pollah in charge this will be the best chance the UO's had to take down the pinnacle of all warlords. With such a massive fighter force, and the firepower of five starships, Pollah believes there is a good chance Narel will be pinned down and taken alive. If not, those same numbers can surely end the life of one being, no matter who it is.

Back on the asteroid, Mace has almost made it to the base of the mysterious mountain. As he closes in on it however the massive storm system which he has been watching for some time is now quickly bearing down on him. The wind has picked up tremendously and eloquent lightning displays are becoming frequent and volatile. The open terrain behind him gives a clear view of these incredible discharges and he even bears witness to the unusually rare phenomenon of ball lightning. Not seeming so rare here, Mace watches the massive spheres of electricity move horizontally, vertically, and even diagonally; always exhibiting erratic actions and behavior before either striking an object or eerily dissipating into nothing. This type of lightning does not seem to seek out the metallic surface of the asteroid as normal bolts would.

Mace arrives below the treacherous mountaintop which slices high into the clouds of the approaching storm. He hides within a small cavern for shelter as the violent weather system bears down. He builds a fire using some rocks and tinder in preparation to rest again for a while in order to avoid the storm. The temperature has dropped significantly during the system's approach and Mace hopes that the trend does not continue as he's now left with little protection from the cold. He lays down near his fire and readies himself to wait it out.

The storm begins with pellet-sized raindrops that fall relentlessly and is soon producing an inch every few minutes when coupled with the runoff from the cliff beside him. The rainfall is unyielding and fails to break for several hours forcing the soldier to do nothing other than sit and wait. Mace's cavern begins to leak and the conditions outside soon become flood-like. As he watches the asteroid's powerful weather capabilities first hand, small mudslides and streams develop off the steeper part of the mountain, yet none seem to directly endanger him. All in all Mace feels fairly protected within his makeshift shelter, except from the cold of course. In regard to the falling temperatures, all the resilient UO officer can do is cling to the hope that the storm passes before he becomes hypothermic. Between the constant and hypnotic sound of running water along with the dark skies and bitter cold, Mace eventually begins to lose all track of time.

As he attempts to stay dry and warm by the fire he hears the rain suddenly stop and moves to the cavern entrance to see if it has passed. As he peers up at the massive cloud formation he witnesses a bundled-up grouping of pure white rain clouds passing over, but another part of the storm approaches just within it's wake. Large gray and green swirling clouds have now moved almost directly overtop of him. Mace watches the spectacular storm formation as it sprouts out tornadoes at will, while slowly passing over the valley spread out before him. The wind picks up with great intensity and large balls of ice, tightly packed together along with sediment that's been carried into the clouds, begin falling freely from the sky. Mace has seen his share of erratic weather, but as far as strange storms go this was a doozy. As the ice balls rain down with great force, Mace turns to go back into his shelter. He doesn't take more than two steps before suddenly being struck in the back of the head by a fist size piece of hail. The solider stumbles into the cavern as his head begins spinning from the blow. He tries to regain his bearings, but the impact was just too much and the soldier collapses to the ground, passing out a few feet from the fire.

Aboard Brutus' command ship he still frantically searches for his missing friend. He sits alone inside his quarters obsessively staring at schematics of the sector.

"I know you're here Mace, where are you?"

He shuffles over the zone layout and data readings from the search mission which have now become a hill-like pile lying atop his desk. He pulls out a batch of freshly taken images from the numerous probe satellites that the fleet has scouring the sector for signs of life. Brutus has already looked over the first fourteen sets of several hundred recorded images and found nothing, it's to the point now that he knows what he's going to look at before his eyes even lay upon the picture. All asteroids and debris within the zone were included in the previous scans so there's no reason to think anything would have changed. Yet, true to his current state Brutus will leave no stone unturned…or re-turned for that matter. He flips through them quickly, scanning for what he's now come to expect, nothing. But this time something is different, one of the images sticks out to him. He focuses in on a small, gas covered asteroid with a nearly untainted atmosphere. Untainted except for one minor blemish, one that he had not seen before, and one that the obsessed soldier would not have missed.

Brutus calls in an analyst, "I need all data on this asteroid and an analysis of this streak immediately."

The analyst hooks into the terminal and quickly accesses the data. "There's no previous reading sir."

"Just like all the others", responds Brutus disheartened.

"No sir", the analyst confusingly replies, "the other readings are negative, this object just shows up as undetermined. It's as though we can't scan it at all. We must have missed it in our broader searches because there is no alert within the system for unknown readings, everything is supposed to get at least a basic, material label of positive or negative."

Brutus replies, "These scanners can break down any material in the Verse given enough time and we've been running them for hours and hours now, how can there be no reading at all?

The analyst shakes his head, "The system is showing one match within the planetary database, an asteroid known as 1166 was discovered inside the Relada System, but was never able to be studied due to this same anomaly."

Brutus responds, "Why do you say was?"

"Because according to this it disappeared over two thousand years ago, its destruction is summarized as obliterated via spontaneous implosion due to the volatile nature of the asteroid's unidentified composition. That's all we have on it sir."

"You still haven't answered my other question, how come our scanners can't analyze it?"

The analyst answers, unsure and confused, "I have no idea sir, but that gas mark looks a lot like the tracer of a ship. It would be a small one, probably a fighter and according to the comparison grid you're right, it wasn't there before. The scanner's memory shows the same area receiving a scan minutes earlier and that streak is
clearly absent."

The analyst looks away from the computer and up at Brutus with uneasy eyes, "For something to just appear like that, within such a small time window and without being detected by the fleet, how can that even be possible. What's going on sir?"

Brutus replies, "I don't know, but we're moving the fleet to that asteroid immediately."

Brutus flips on the video link and alerts his pilots, "Change coordinates to 186-AA-47, only known reference point to target appears in our database as asteroid 1166 and these specs aren't reliable. Just prepare to land on the strange-looking, cloud-covered asteroid."

The pilots acknowledge the change and alter course. Brutus returns to the analyst and continues investigating this well-deserved lead.

A few minutes into the trip, Sergeant Tailkon storms into Brutus' quarters and smugly asks, "Could you answer your video link commanding Sergeant, Major Veela would like to have a word with you."

This particular UO Major is a female Luvyian who plays strict favorites with her subordinates, Sergeant Tailkon just happens to be her most beloved pupil. She has tremendous political influence within the UO and would be a lock for Commander one day except for her lack of experience on the battlefield.

Brutus gives Tailkon a disgusted look as he walks over to the video link. He knows Veela loves to impose her will on those her people set their sights on, and at the moment that would seem to be Brutus. Still determined, he remains unwavering as he moves over and glances into the video link, "Major Veela, I wasn't aware you were involved in this mission, after all it has been sanctioned by the council and I have full authority over it".

The Major replies with the tone of a dictator, "Not any more. After Sergeant Tailkon informed me that you've been wasting UO resources in order to continue a mission that should have never takin place to begin with and has produced no reason for continuation, I went to Commander Blenko who authorized me to shut you down. The explanation on record will show that this determination was made due to lack of progress. So under these revised Commander's orders you are hereby summoned to return your fleet to Utopera at once."

While Veela attempted to continue her flex of power, Brutus rips the Video Link's power cables from the wall.

Sergeant Tailkon now becomes hostile, "What do ya think you're doing Callous?"

He pulls out and opens his plasma staff, but Brutus dodges the Sergeant and bluntly strikes him over the head with his own, unopened staff. Tailkon is knocked unconscious and falls to the floor like a brick of gold. The analyst jumps back against the wall in shock.

"Why did you do that", he apprehensively asks Brutus.

"Because you and I both know that something is going on here and Tailkon won't stop until he ruins this mission. You know those aren't coincidences with the Radus and this asteroid. Radus systems don't just miss things and neither would our entire fleet. Mace's ship went down on that rock and he's still there. I'm sure you haven't forgotten when Lieutenant Crimson saved that Galaen Charter from the Org extermination squads, you had family on that ship right?"

"So what am I supposed to do, help you with mutiny?" The analyst replies.

"It's not mutiny because I am the commanding officer." Brutus calmly pleads, "I'm also the only one Tailkin can definitively say disobeyed him. I will accept all the repercussions if you agree to help and never speak of your involvement to anyone, you have my word."

The analyst hesitantly replies, "Fine. I haven't forgotten what I owe Mace, what we all owe him really, and I never will. I'll do whatever you need me to."

"Good", responds Brutus, "for now lock Sergeant Tailkon in the bathroom and inject him with a tranquillizer from the medical bay, 2 ccs of dizene should work nicely, that'll keep him out for at least a few hours. I'll get the fleet on course and hopefully we'll find Mace before Major Veela can get the inevitable retrieval units out here."

Down on the asteroid Mace awakens from his undesired nap which ends up lasting several hours. As his eyes open, the soldier can immediately see that the temperature must have continued to plummet as the ground is now covered with several feet of snow and ice. The storm was gone, but it turned the once habitable plateau into an arctic tundra. Never before had Mace seen such drastic climate variation. He must have just lied there through it all, curled into a ball as his unconscious body tried desperately to retain any heat it could. The fire has been smothered by the cold for some time and is now nothing more than a frozen heap of charred logs. He attempts to move from his cramped position only to feel extreme pain shoot rampantly throughout his body. He now notices that he cannot feel the extreme cold on his skin, as a matter of fact he can't really feel his skin at all. As hard as he struggles, the soldier cannot break free from his cramped position and Mace realizes that he must be suffering from severe frostbite. His neck, back, arms, legs, and parts of his face have all become fully necrotic and his skin has turned to a deep purple, almost black color. The brave soldier tries to push through the pain repeatedly, yet time after time he cannot overcome the unbearable agony the condition has caused. He retains minimal control over his joints, but each limb has been pushed far past the freezing point and any motion only causes further damage. His screams echo off the mountainside, yet his desperate attempts make no progress. As he sees blood start leaking from the numerous patches of frostbitten skin, Mace realizes that his efforts are useless. The effected area covers far too much of his body and successfully moving out of the current position would surely kill him. It appears as though there is no escape for the brave soldier this time, asteroid 1166 seems to have given him an unavoidable death sentence. Crimson looks to the exit of his cavern and breathes deeply as he peers out onto the vast, now snow-covered plains. It looks as though this will be the last spectacular site he gazes upon. Mace calms himself more and more, attempting to drown out the pain by relaxing his mind.

He continues this for some time, staring into oblivion and strangely feeling more at ease with every moment that passes. Lying there, stuck within the desolate silence emanating from the aftermath of the storm, an eerie tranquility passes over him. The snowflakes seem to fall in perfect formation, the wind swirls around in an all too predictable manner, and the clouds above shift and intersect with purpose and precision. The harmony he feels at this moment is similar to how he felt sitting beside the lake, earlier on in his journey. Mace has never been afraid to die, not since he was a small child anyway, and now in what seems like a hopeless situation he will not shorten nor ruin his remaining time with panic or fear. He simply embraces his fate and sees only beauty in the place that has seemed to condemn him from the start.

Suddenly, he comes out of this trance as an idea comes to mind and looks upon the iced-over fire with overflowing intent. Maybe he could use his new found ability to speed up the particles within his tissues, just opposite of the way he manipulated the atoms at the lake. With the state that the affected areas are in, it's obvious that even the tiniest particles have been incapacitated by the cold, reversing this process may restore them enough to heal.

First he decides to focus on his back, this also happens to be the largest area affected by the deadly frostbite and therefore probably the best to sample on. He envisions himself lying within the cavern and soon views himself, looking upon his body from a complete third-person perspective. Mace looks closely at his back through this out-of-body view, and with a little more concentration he's able to see the atoms and particles within. Most of the particles have stopped moving entirely, so Mace focuses even harder and illuminates the subatomic particles of his skin and muscles. Some of these particles have also come to a complete stop, and the rest are barely moving. The desperate soldier knows he'll have to act fast. He attempts to speed them up, but after his first few tries nothing happens, the pain even increasing some. For a moment, he questions whether or not this is even possible.

After a brief bout with indecision, Mace releases his frustration and increases his focus with all the energy he has.

A few more minutes pass when suddenly the particles show signs that they may finally budge. Those already moving gradually begin to speed up, and soon after those which are stuck begin to break free and gain momentum. The muscles and tissue that appear damaged slowly show signs of healing and reconstruction. Was this all in Mace's head or was this somehow really happening? The more the particles move the easier it becomes to increase their speed and Mace now starts to feel some sensation in his back once again. At first he is met with intense discomfort and distress, but as he presses on and continues to focus, the pain is relieved and the skin on his back is left with only some minor, burn-like blemishes.

As he finishes with his back, Mace straightens out from his curled position and relieves some of the tension which had built up and become significant during his freeze. The relief is unparalleled and well-deserved, he lies there calmly for a moment until the pain from the other afflicted areas abruptly sets back into mind. He again begins the unfreezing process, and continues until he's repaired every part of his body. Once he is nearly fully restored, he sits up, taking deep breathes to fully regain himself. Oddly enough, he only feels fatigued briefly until yet another wind of energy hits the soldier once he relaxes for a bit.

After a short rest he's on his feet with only a few cuts and cold burns from the ordeal. Mace looks over his rejuvenated body just before he leaves the cavern, now feeling prepared for his redemption against this strange world and the being who's forsaken him here without cause. The soldier shakes the ice off his armor and suits up to climb the mountain. He walks out of his cavern and up to the steep
mountainside which is now covered with several inches of ice.

Mace looks to the mountaintop which almost feels as though it is taunting him and says to himself with a peculiar smirk, "You're not gonna stop me".

He then jumps to a small perch and begins his climb. He kicks and cuts into the ice, using the jagged joints of his armor for traction. He also finds another use for his new-found skills, melting hand and foot holes wherever they're needed. He slips a few times, but it is clear that this overtly resilient human will not be denied with only a few thousand feet between him and his goal.

Over on Prospina, Narel meditates within the confines of his private suite. It has a spectacular view of the glorious city, although he's chosen to close the automated blinds, sitting in almost complete darkness. The warlord relaxes within the silence, combing through the thoughts of a great and unpredictable mind. He still awaits the completion of repairs on the Malacaus, which after his adamant demands should soon be approaching. The video link suddenly begins to sound off and Narel sighs as he breaks his concentration, standing to answer it. He opens the link and a scrambled image appears on the screen. Both image and voice are unidentifiable, but the figure assertively informs Narel of the situation developing on Prospina.

Narel stares at the screen as if he knows who he's looking at, the scrambled voice exclaims, "You need to get off Prospina now!"

"Why is your feed scrambled?" Narel replies.

The anonymous figure responds, "Because the UO has tracked you there and they could be monitoring this very call. A civilian-dressed team spotted you upon arrival. There is a more than formidable fleet headed your way as we speak and they are not far off. I just found out myself or I would have notified you sooner. You've made a rare mistake lord Narel, don't let it be your end. Get out now!"

Narel immediately closes the video link and rushes out of his room and back to the transport vessel. He flies the small, pod-like craft aggressively through the Prospina skies, dangerously cutting through the civilian skyways as he maneuvers his way back to the low orbit repair station. He races through the traffic of the automated shuttle ways, cutting off the synchronized flight plans of transport shuttles and causing an array of crashes and near-collision situations before quickly moving on. Debris falls as parachutes and airbags open up throughout the warlord's wake.

Upon reaching the repair station, Narel quickly parks his transport ship and exits. This time he makes little attempt to blend in with the crowd and moves hastily back towards repair bay 28b to reclaim his starship and make his escape.

UO privates Uren and Gaaron witness Narel exiting his transport knowing they still haven't received word from Commander Pollah.

Uren looks to his partner, "We may need to engage him, we still haven't gotten word and the fleet needs every second they can get."

"I know", Gaaron replies, "We can't let this chance slip away."

As they prepare to attack their video link receives the much anticipated call from Commander Pollah. "We've just arrived within Prospina's high orbit, we'll have the station surrounded shortly."

"That's great sir", replies Uren, "Narel is headed to his ship now and he seems to be in a rush. Should we pursue?"

Pollah replies, "No, I don't see any reason for the two of you to confront that lunatic alone when we have his exit entirely cut off, it isn't worth the risk."

"I understand Commander. We'll await the results of your encounter."

"We'll get em for ya", Commander Pollah replies, "good work soldiers."

Uren closes the video link and looks up, he says to Gaaron, "Where'd he go?"

Private Gaaron looks through the busy crowd, "I don't know he was just over there, near the betha stand."

As they both scan the crowd for their unmistakable enemy, Uren hears a plasma staff open directly behind them. He and Gaaron try to turn quickly, but they are already outdone. Narel cuts Private Gaaron across the abdomen and Uren across the throat with one devastating diagonal stroke. Gaaron survives the first slice and manages to open her staff as her partner falls to the ground dead. Narel blocks the wounded soldier's weak attack however, and he beheads Gaaron in front of over a dozen witnesses. People scream and some begin to panic, but the repair station is so loud and overcrowded that only those directly surrounding the assault even know it took place.

"Tell that to your commander, cowards!" says the warlord as he stands over the pair of lifeless bodies.

Narel then re-covers his face, which was exposed during the fight and disappears into the crowd, rushing back towards the Malacaus.

Upon boarding his ship he yells to the crew, "Break for open space and prepare to use interstellar thrusters!"

A worker from the Prospina repair team approaches Narel, "We're not finished yet, the…"

Narel interupts, "Are the interstellar systems operational?"

The worker replies, "Yes, but…"

Without hesitation, Narel throws the worker off the ship, which is elevated several hundred feet above the hangar floor. He yells to his crew again, "Get us off this station!"

The order spreads quickly and within a few minutes the ship is pulling away from the docking station. Narel rushes to the bridge as they prepare for departure. Dozens if not hundreds of workers from Prospina's docking station cannot evacuate the ship in time. It quickly breaks away from the station with no clearance and very little warning, leaving most of the docking station repair teams stranded aboard the massive vessel.

The mammoth Malacaus breaks out of Prospina's atmosphere with blatant disregard of the civilian skyways, causing an even more chaotic traffic scene than Narel had been responsible for on the planet below. Numerous hazardous accidents occur as small personal spacecraft as well as transport ships hazardously evade or crash directly into the massive Nexcin warship. The civilian aircraft flying about are miniscule in comparison to Narel's prized goliath, thus their collisions don't even pierce its bulky outer shielding. The impacts can only be seen as fleeting explosions bursting and deflecting off the ship like insects on a windshield.

As the Malacaus breaches lower orbit and breaks for open space, Narel gets his first glimpse of the UO blockade up ahead. It is immediately clear that even with the many advantages of the Malacaus, it is still only one ship and the warlord is overtly outnumbered. Still, they continue ahead at full speed.

His captain says, "Should we evade?"

Narel looks over the blockade as the five UO starships sit in perfect formation, just waiting for a reason to release their fighters. He replies, "No, dispatch all fighter squadrons and split the entire attack force into two groups, each will engage an enemy starship on opposing ends of the UO formation. Let the detachment leaders know to strike in unison and concentrate maximum fire onto their designated target as soon as scopes are within range. After you brief the squadron leaders turn the Malacaus' radiation and thermal shielding to full strength, we're going straight through the center of that blockade.

Aboard Commander Pollah's starship, he watches the Malacuas as it approaches the blockade with no change of speed nor diversion of flight course.

A lieutenant asks the Commander, "Why isn't he evading, he can't possibly plan to attack us head on? They're outnumbered five to one."

Commander Pollah replies, "I don't know Narel, but from what I've heard he's not the type to be captured. Spread out the fleet and prepare for a general assualt, that ship looks like it can take a beating so cue up all missile bays and stand by to pursue after the original strike."

Nexcin fighters soon reach the outer starships and begin an aggressive attack. The UO fleet's anti-missile turrets engage and defend while their own fighters are slowly released. The Nexcins target AMT installations and docking areas to inhibit UO defenses. A space battle rages on opposite sides of the UO fleet, but Narel's forces are not inflicting any overwhelming damage. The Nexcin fighters are many, but they are no match for starship defenses and will not last long attacking in such a way. If all his fighters are destroyed, Narel will be a sitting duck for the UO fleet and the Malacaus will become target practice.

Commander Pollah puts on a communication headset and speaks to the commanding officers of his other starships. "All ships spread to launch formation and prepare to fire 2 waves of devastators; that should take a nice chuck out of that monstrosity and hopefully disable it. If we can get them offline, keep the flank secure while my team does the boarding. Make sure they stay surrounded at all times."

As the gap between the Malacaus and the UO fleet quickly closes, it's looking like this is going to turn into a full-blown dog fight. The UO formation begins to spread out, but Narel has anticipated this move and it's the one he's been waiting for. He instantly strikes, yelling to his captain, "Fire all fusors and nukes, with a majority solution targeting the center ships. As soon as the missiles reach their mark, hit the interstellar thrusters."

"But my lord", the captain replies with distress, "if the detonations don't kill us, that amount of radiation surely will."

Narel turns to face the soldier, giving him an aggravated stare, "I would never give an order that would sacrifice my own life, now do it."

The captain fires all 97 high-yield warheads currently aboard the Malacaus straight towards the UO fleet, which is now less than fifty starship-lengths away.

The Malacaus is so close when it releases the missiles that the UO fleet has barely any time to react.

Commander Pollah yells out, "Fire cryo-rounds, fire cryo-rounds."

All UO starships attempt to send out interceptor missiles and spray cryo-rounds to destroy the warheads, but there just isn't enough time. The UO's advanced counter tactics disable over half of them, but nearly fifty fission and fusion detonations make it through and blast into the fleet. The barrage hits the starships with devastating force, erupting in a nuclear display that looks almost as bright as a supernova to the civilians down on Prospina. The spectacle was unlike anything they had ever seen before, and many Prospinians feared that a cosmic disaster was under way.

The reality of the situation was nearly as devastating, at least it was for the UO. Three UO starships including Commander Pollah's are entirely obliterated. The remaining two are the corner ships of the formation, those which were targeted heavily by the Nexcin fighter squadrons just before Narel's superblast took the majority of his own fighters out as well. Due to Commander Pollah's order to spread out, these two starship's survive the blast. Unfortunately, they take serious damage from the intense fighter bombardments, as well as the nuclear blast waves, leaving their crews in disarray. As the explosions cease, Narel orders his ship to fire all thrusters and pass straight through the aftermath of the detonations. His captain reluctantly does so. The Malacuas barrels through the debris and fallout of the irradiated catastrophe as the thrusters begin to fire rapidly, propelling the immense murder machine towards interstellar speed. The mostly Nexcin crew hangs on as the colossal ship breaks through the debris field with great velocity and unbreakable momentum. Their screams can almost be heard over the sound of the thrusters, operating at full throttle as they pass through the unimaginably hazardous fallout zone. With every inch the ship moves, they are pushed through intense waves of heat and radiation. The Malacaus seems to have received sufficient enough repairs to remain functional and it's quickly out of range for what's left of the badly disabled UO fleet. The battered pair of surviving UO starships do not attempt to engage him any further. Instead the wounded remnants of Commander Pollah's fleet are forced to call Utopera for a rescue team as the warlord's warship limps off, escaping into the depths of the Verse once again.

As the UO begins to deal with the tragedy just caused by Narel, Mace's ordeal on the strange asteroid still continues. He's climbed nearly three quarters of the way up the mountain, pushing himself harder with each meter he climbs. The winds ripping across the cliff face are intense and with nearly every step the determined soldier struggles to maintain his grip. The mountainside is nearly vertical at this point and more difficult to overcome than any climb Mace has ever encountered.

He continues to pound and melt himself support holes, until while looking up desperately, he spots a ledge just above him. Mace makes his way over to it and climbs up onto the rough edge of an icy shelf which reveals a flat, snow-covered landing. Across the fairly long landing lies a large, deep cave into which he can see only blackness. There is a fire burning inside a well-designed, seemingly ancient pit just in front of the cave entrance and fairly large footprints pressed into the snow along the area all around it. Mace approaches the cave cautiously and as he reaches the fire pit he can see symbols painted beneath the layers of ice covering the outside of the cavern. It appears as though the strange being has inhabited this cave for some time. As Mace nears the fire, the large entity appears next to him, seemingly out of nowhere and knocks the tired soldier to the ground.

Mace slides to a stop as his unknown adversary stands over the soldier with a disturbed expression, drooling as he takes deep, agitated breathes. It speaks with an angry tone at first, "I give you extra time added to your pathetic life and you follow me back to my home. Is it not clear that you should fear your encounter with me?"

Mace replies, "I do not fear something simply because it is stronger than me. I am who I am and that's not going to change in a matter of days. You are clearly more powerful than I, but if we are going to fight to the death it's gonna to be here and its gonna be now."

The being backs off slightly, now replying in a much calmer voice, "I am impressed you even made it here, especially in such a short time. I guess you should be commended for such survival skills and ingenuity, you must be quite resourceful. Have you learned nothing about this place during your shortened stay?"

"Only that it shouldn't even exist", Mace responds, "the climate, wildlife, and even gravity conditions….they can't be possible." He looks around the strange world, "Believe me, I wouldn't have landed here by choice."

"And yet, you're here anyway." It replies, "all useful knowledge and common instincts, things that you are certain of and have always held true tell you that this place is impossible. It simply can't exist, and yet it does. The truth is, this place is the realest, most influential spot in the Verse. All of the knowledge and answers about life, nature, purpose; the very progression of our accumulated existence can be found here. You will never be as alive or as free as you are right now."

The being looks out at the asteroid as the winds calm for a moment, "I know you can feel it, because I have since the first day I set foot on this place. There's something incredible, something divine that imprints itself onto you, penetrating to your very core. Only the chosen are brought here my friend and only when it is believed that they are ready."

"Chosen by who?" Mace replies.

The being laughs mockingly, "By the Verse of course, the creator of all matter and life."

Mace gives an uncertain look before responding, "I don't know what types of plants you've been eating out here or if maybe being stuck alone on this galactic island has gotten to your brain, but the Verse is no more alive than a rock or even a planet for that matter."

"Don't be so certain", the being replies, "I assure you that the Verse is very much alive, and I wouldn't be so sure about all individual planets out there either."

Mace somewhat arrogantly says back, "The Universe is simply a puzzle, everything from a snowflake to you and I has a self-defined purpose within it, but that is all. The pieces have just happened to fall this way, they weren't placed here by anything."

"That's not entirely true", the entity replies, "the Verse is as premeditated as a command passed down from your UO council. I'm sure you believe in them, the greatest of the great, although as we all will soon see they are as susceptible to influence as any group or being. Back to the point however, from the time of it's eruption into existence, the Verse has watched over all."

The being raises his arm, using telekinesis to lift several rocks and ice chunks into the air. He repositions the debris into the shape of an early galaxy or solar cluster and uses them as a visual aid while continuing.

"In the beginning, when the Verse was still very young, it had a great influence over every action that took place within itself. A small push here or a shift there could determine whether a formation of matter would inevitably turn into a black hole or a binary star system, whether a debris pile would become a comet or a planet, whether a nebula evolves slowly into a main sequence star or jumps forward in its life cycle and becomes a red giant or white dwarf within a matter of millennia. The Verse created all things and did so with an undeniable purpose. This one true ideal of the Verse was slow and challenging to say the least, yet through extensive trial and error it would one day yield the perfect byproduct, life...

As the being drops his visual of the developing universe, he holds out his hand and allows several insects and small creatures to land upon his arm. Mace is amazed as he hadn't seen any sign of life upon the soaring heights of this frozen mountaintop, nor did he think anything could survive, other than the two of them of course. Still, dozens of creatures flock to the mysterious being as if they were called or summoned to him.

The strange entity continues, "but even the all encompassing Universe could not perfect life. Species still die off, worlds are destroyed by various causes, and even the advanced races of the Verse plague each other with war and greed. You see, the Universe strives to create life, it is the ultimate achievement and therefore it also wishes to protect its natural offspring by any means within it's power."

Mace thinks before answering, "So your telling me that the Verse has a consciousness of it's own and can see everything that goes on here."

"It doesn't necessarily see", the entity replies, "but yes it observes all."

Mace ponders a moment, surprisingly now becoming engrossed in the conversation, "It just doesn't make sense. If the Universe cares so much about it's inhabitants, then why doesn't the all powerful Verse intercede during times of genocide, famine, plague, galactic war, or the million or so other atrocities that have occurred to the hundreds of races over the past few thousand centuries. Not only that, but a conscious creator would have unlimited power and influence; so why not interact with it's prized creation, even if for no other reason than to show us the way?"

"It doesn't work like that", the entity responds, "we literally are the Universe. It flows through your atoms while it also makes up their composition, it does not take any single body because it is everybody and everything....every particle and every force. Most directly put, the Verse observes us within itself. You, me, it, that, them, those, every and all that we see and even that which we don't is the Verse. We are simply the subconscious parts of a conscious   whole;   living   our   existence   within   its existence....sometimes seeming like more of a parasite than the symbionts we should be."

The being turns and walks back towards the fire. "Let me tell you a little story, one that may shed a bit of light on the Verse as you know it."

Mace's thoughts quickly jump back to his true objective and he rudely interrupts, "Look, I didn't come up here to listen to your stories, I came to find my way out."

The being silences him, "You'll get your chance to face me soon enough, but listen to what I say and perhaps you'll be enlightened. Who knows you may even survive if you prove me wrong. Always be cautious of the present soldier, what can be learned may save you in the future, short or long term."

Mace isn't sure why, but as much as he wants to get off this asteroid something compels him to listen, "Fine, say your piece."

The being relaxes and paces in front of the fire as it speaks, "I'm sure you know of a race called the Colton?"

"Of course", Mace replies, "they're probably the most advanced and sophisticated species in the Verse, who wouldn't know of them."

The entity continues, "I apologize, many races weren't as acknowledged in my time. Around five millennia ago, due to a combination of surging technology and social boredom, the Colton decided that they would genetically engineer the perfect race. One that would compliment the rest of the Verse quite adequately, while simultaneously allowing their creators to reap the pride and reputation of engineering this tremendous feat. A race of the finest, smartest, strongest, and mentally toughest individuals ever bred. The species would be given a home planet and once genetically coded to survive such a planet they would be left on their own to develop as a culture. This was believed by the Colton to be a natural way of introducing artificial life to the Verse."

Mace cuts in, "Genetic tampering like you're referring is banned by every Universal alliance I can think of. The Colton never would have attempted such an experiment."

The entity impatiently snaps back, "It wasn't at the time, now don't interrupt and just listen! As planned, the race truly was left on their own as the Colton watched over their creation from a distance. The young, yet superior species thrived extensively for the first century of its existence, quickly coming together as a group and establishing an identity for themselves. Numerous tribes mastered the individual geographical territories of the planet and two centuries into their development they had established a primitive, yet stable infrastructure with a uniform language and currency system. Although the planet's geography had broken them into nearly a dozen separate tribes, each individual sect seemed to trade and coexist peacefully. They were coming together as a whole and discovering the bountiful resources that their planet had to offer. The young race develops pride and their early organizational skills exceed even the Colton's expectations. Primitive monuments and large-scale wonders are created with great care, detail, and craftsmanship; outlining early settlements and attesting to the races camaraderie and teamwork.

By the start of their third century the budding civilization had united as a people and the entire world was at peace. Over the next few decades they built vast cities and technology started climbing at a magnanimous rate. The Colton looked on with pride and wonder until about halfway through the fourth century of their experiment when, if ever, would the super race hit an unforeseen obstacle. The time had finally come in their four hundred and forty-fifth year of existence. You see, when the Colton created them they gave their prized creation a nearly invulnerable immune system; no allergies, no disease, no ailments of any kind. A privilege that held true for the super race over nearly four and a half centuries. Around this time however, several members of the race begin to suddenly exhibit odd health symptoms; bleeding from orifices, extreme body aches, and also high fevers. The problem seemed mild enough, but the affliction spreads moderately over time and scientists soon began a campaign to analyze the situation. The extremely intelligent race puzzled over the anomalous disease and as time continues to go by the sick did not get better, they became much worse. The pain and bleeding increases as the victim's muscles begin to deteriorate from within. Eventually, if the patient doesn't bleed to death, they die from either severe organ necrosis or internal hemorrhage. As you can imagine, panic quickly spreads throughout the previously utopian cities and the prodigal race of the Verse desperately seeks a cure for the enigmatic disease. For the first time in their history, the species would have to closely examine their constitution and anatomy. As they test and experiment in hopes of creating a miracle vaccine, a substantial portion of their population dies off with each passing day. Eventually, after months of testing the vaccine is finished at last, however by the time it's completed over seventy percent of their world's population is dead and the casualties have nearly ceased. Most of the remaining thirty percent seemed to be over or have at least developed an immunity to the plague, yet fear still leads the survivor's top remaining scientists to complete and release the vaccine anyway, as a supposed precautionary measure. A few paranoid groups step up and protest the release, but fear inevitably leads the survivors to ok it. It is distributed to the masses through clinics along with an airborne strain that is released to rid the atmosphere of the virus. The results of this move are the most horrific of all. The airborne vaccine almost immediately mutates into an immensely more dangerous version of the deadly pandemic. Within five cycles, the entire race would be a casualty of the superstrain, which in tragic irony was created by their own scientists. The race that was supposed to be the epitome of perfection, a breed that was engineered to be absolutely faultless; a species that was to lead the rest of the inhabitants of the Verse to harmony and unity had now been eradicated just as suddenly as they were conceived. And from what? Not through war, imperialism, or catastrophe; not over aggression, greed, or arrogance; but simple natural selection. The perfect race had been ended by a microbe, silenced by a killer smaller than even their ever-so-powerful eyes could see.

The Colton were devastated by the loss and they came to the determination that no race would ever be capable of engineering life, this was what led to the first genetic tampering alliance along with the now popular belief that creating intelligent civilization is simply too complex. Any attempt to create a civilized species from this point on would be considered a heinous and immoral act.

Mace chimes in, "That's a fascinating story, but is this really supposed to make me believe that all of us were created through some master plan of the Universe?"

The being resents Maces skepticism, yet it remains calm; "I haven't come to the fascinating part yet, be patient. You see after they're creation died off, the planet was abandoned by the Colton, as they no longer had any suitable use for it. They left it vacant for centuries until nearly a millennium later when a scouting party was sent back to search and scan the planet for an inventory of obtainable resources. What they found was astonishing. A new species was in the early stages of evolution and had spread across a majority of the planet; the supremely intelligent Colton Race was baffled at the finding. Upon further examination, the dna of the new species was quite similar to the original inhabitants whom had now been long extinct. There were a few alterations of course, most importantly the immune system of the new species was now in sync with the planet, the Colton noticed that they had developed a new vital organ all together. Once inspected and analyzed it was revealed that the organ was a detoxification gland that aided the immune system immensely in filtering out harmful bacteria and toxins naturally- found within their environment. The find further influenced the Colton beliefs that the natural processes of the Verse are the only means of creating life and led to the formation of their diamond-solid genetic engineering laws that would eventually be adopted all over the Verse. The newly evolved race which was reborn and took over the Colton planet are known to you today as the Artilonians.

Mace's expression shows that he is somewhat compelled by the story although he remains skeptical, "If that is in fact true then it's astonishing, but I think it shows the perseverance that a species must have to survive the trials of nature more so than it proves your theory. I respect the Verse as much as anyone, but to believe that it is self aware and proactive about our faulty at best existence is foolish to say the least."

"I knew you were not him", the entity replies, "you would be able to see the Verse as it is. I've tried to give you perspective, but now you'll get what you came up here for. You presume far too much young one, and you lack faith. Prepare to fight."

Mace replies, "It's your idea not mine, I just wanna get outta here."

The large gray being moves to his position, but Mace is stunned to see that his adversary doesn't seem to shift and step as quickly as usual. Mace can actually follow his movements now, and his enemy doesn't seem to be doing this intentionally. The alien creature gives young Crimson a death stare, similar to the way gladiators within the gambling belts do just before a duel inside the arenas. It then lets out a deafening war cry just before lunging towards him.

The crafty soldier is prepared for the impact and puts all his weight into his enemy. As they collide a large shockwave stretches out and knocks large deposits of snow and sediment off the mountaintop, the force of the collision pushes Mace back and he slides on his backside across the icy surface.

The being yells out, "You are actually quite powerful my friend, it seems I've underestimated you. But you are still not as strong as I....and you're definitely not him."

A frustrated Mace replies, "Not who?"

The being answers condescendingly, "You should have explored this place with a little more interest if you'd like to know its secrets."

The being stands tall just before attacking Mace again, this time Crimson can see him with even greater clarity and it almost feels as though time is slowing down for the soldier. Mace waits until just before the creature makes contact, then he swiftly ducks the charging assailant and flips him over his head using the being's own tremendous momentum against him. The attacker is propelled through the air and does several flips head over feet before grabbing a rock and spectacularly pulling himself down to the ground. The being somehow manages to land on his feet and slides to a stop. Without any hesitation it runs straight back at Mace full speed. As he approaches with even further aggression, the being drops to his side and slides under Mace's legs extending his arms to knock both feet out from under him. The gray warrior then quickly jumps to his feet and kneels overtop of Mace, pinning him down. He then wastes no time, taking huge swings at the helpless soldier with tremendous force, pounding craters into the rocks and mountainside beneath his feet. Mace squirms and shifts amidst the alien's clutches, dodging one punch after the other as just one of these brutal hits landing upon their intended target would prove to be fatal. The creature's arms seem to have the strength of a lead and tungsten alloy, as collisions with the rocky mountain surface do little damage to his flesh.

The being continues to miss and shifts his weight for a split second to reposition himself; as he does Mace focuses his mind on pushing the being off of him with all his might. The fatigued UO soldier feels a last second adrenaline boost that miraculously works as the powerful creature is knocked off of him. The entity rolls backwards, but quickly pops up once again, this time with a shocked and perplexed look upon his face. It now occurs to Mace that he knocked the being back without ever even touching him...he must've done it telekinetically.

The being shouts out, "You must have learned more from your stay than I thought."

Mace raises his hand again to attempt the same trick, but this time the being is ready for it. He puts his hands up as well and Mace can feel the energy being pushed back at him. Before he can counter further, the soldier is overwhelmed by his powerful adversary. It seems that just as one can influence particles to move, speed up, or slow down with their mind, the process can reversed by someone who can also manipulate them. Mace is knocked back into the wall and the creature pins him against it telekinetically. In a crude display of power, the beast heats the wall up behind him in seconds, causing the rock to become red hot and burn Mace in several places. He then releases the soldier from the wall and focuses it's attention to the snowfall covering the mountain. The being telekinetically lifts up dozens of small pieces of debris from all over the landing and maliciously sends a barrage of ice chunks and rock at the injured Crimson. They rip and tear over his body like an intense hail storm as the being hits him relentlessly with the ruthless attack. Mace is soon cut all over; bleeding and burnt, he fights mentally with all his will to slow down the attack, concentrating with everything he has, but the entity controls too strong of a command over the debris field. The stoning continues for several minutes without the slightest decrease in intensity. It seems as though the strange gray entity believed this would kill Mace, but the soldier is persistent enough to tire the creature out. The beast eventually stops the onslaught and gasps for breathe, ill-wisely showing his own fatigue. It then walks over to the beleaguered soldier slowly, lifts Mace up and slams him into the mountainside before tossing him towards the edge of the landing. Mace slides to within inches of the cliff's edge.

The creature yells out, "Now you die false prophet!"

Mace lays there weakened and beaten, the winds rip across his injured body as he sees his enemy approaching for the kill. It walks over with condescending laughter and the overconfidence to match. He stands a few feet from Mace and prepares to finish him off. As the being winds up to kick him off the mountainside, Mace lies motionless on the ground, seemingly defeated. At the last possible moment, Mace reaches out and grabs both of the creature's legs. With all of the will he has left in his body, Mace focuses on stopping the particles moving throughout the beings lower extremities. Within seconds, both it's legs are frozen solid. It tries to stop the process like before, but Mace was too quick and his legs are already frozen into the icy ground. Mace rolls away from the cliff edge, jumps to his feet and says, "Guess you aren't as strong as you thought".

He then puts all his might into a two handed blow to the chest of his large gray nemesis which effectively breaks him in half and knocks his upper body off the mountaintop. He watches the being fall to it's death, giving him back an eerily tranquil stare all the way down. Mace had won the duel, but how would he ever get off this mountaintop, let alone the asteroid.

As he lies there, now beginning to feel the pain of his wounds kick in and unsure of what to do next, he sees an ominous sight that the soldier at first thinks must be an illusion. It was a UO ship, breaking through the asteroid's thick atmosphere. Brutus had done it, he found his friend.

Once realizing the sight to be true, Mace turns to his deceased adversary's fire. He steadies his concentration, which is now becoming easier, and pulls all the unused logs and tinder scattered atop the landing into a pile within the fire pit. He then uses his abilities to turn the heap of wood and debris into an inferno large enough for any ship or scanner to spot. With the signal fire blazing, he drops down onto his back letting out an exhausted breathe, and lies in the snow while his ride makes it's descent.

On board Brutus' ship, the thermal scanners quickly pick up the fire atop the otherwise frozen mountaintop and they make their way over to Mace. The enduring soldier is mentally and physically drained, he is relieved to see that this ordeal seems to finally be over and calmly awaits his retrieval.

The cruiser has some limited trouble with it's instruments and primary systems upon entering the asteroid's strange atmosphere, but after a few moments they come back online. The turbulent skies are difficult to navigate, but UO pilots are the best at what they do and Brutus doesn't have the slightest reservation about hastening the rescue.

Brutus orders his flight team, "Avoid all indicators, take us down as close as you can to the summit without jeopardizing the hover stabilizers. As long as we don't face a hull breech from the turbulence we'll pull him up with a pod line."

"Yes sir", responds the pilot, "Takin her down."

Shearing winds make it impossible for a smaller ship to go down and pick him up, so a transport pod is attached to the cruiser by a long, tension diversion cable which is then lowered down to him. The pod flails somewhat in the inclement weather, but the line holds steady and soon reaches the landing. Mace walks over to and hops inside the small shuttle. Once secured, he's quickly zipped up the long cable and pulled safely onto the ship.

As he boards, Brutus, Arilla, and several other crew members await. The door opens and a battered Mace falls out of the cramped shuttle cockpit. Brutus catches him as he drops and yells for the medic to prepare a bed. Mace looks to Brutus, barely conscious at
this point, "I thought you were goin home?"

"I was", Brutus replies, "but then I thought to myself how often is it that I get to save your ass?"

"We weren't missin this for anything", adds Arilla.

Mace smiles as he is helped up and escorted over to the medical bay, then says to them both, "Thanks for comin".

"No Problem" says Brutus, "I'll never let you live it down. Now rest up, its been a hell of a day."

Mace is escorted away to be treated as Brutus goes back to his quarters and prepares to face the repercussions of his recent actions upon return to Utopera. Brutus' present feelings warrant his earlier decision, seeing Mace alive and safe are well worth the possibility of exile from the order, or even a prison sentence if the Council deems it necessary. The truth is, if Brutus had not made his stand and acted against Sergeant Tailkin, the young officer would have regretted the inaction for the rest of his life. Although he will almost certainly be punished for his handling of the situation, the loyal UO soldier would have never forgiven himself had something happened to Mace, nor would he be able to live with that circumstance for the remainder of his years. To a true friend, it doesn't seem like this was even a choice.

Far off in the Verse, Narel returns to his hidden fleet. He refuses to dock up, ordering a transport pod be sent out to the Malacaus which will chauffer him back to the fleet's flagship. A pod is immediately dispatched to retrieve the warlord, and once transported back he stumbles off the pod to his number 2 in command, Demos Bellerus. Several Nexcins attempt to help their leader to which Narel shouts, "Get off me you taureds!"

The powerful warlord seems to be extremely weakened from the radiation exposure and there are visible burns all over his body.

The Renondin Warrior and Nexcin General walks with Narel, Bellerus soon asks, "What happened my lord?"

His ruler and mentor replies, "I was ambushed by a UO fleet."

"Should we retaliate?" Demos assertively responds.

"No", Narel answers calmly, "destroy the Malacaus, it's become irradiated and is of no use to us."

"What of the crew?" Demos replies.

Narel answers, "I could barely take the level of radiation myself, they're surely dead. Dispose of it quickly, I need time to regain my strength and redetermine our path. I'm not to be disturbed for anything; keep operations in order for now Demos."

He staggers back to his quarters, a strange sight to Demos who has never seen his leader weakened before. He eventually replies, "Of course my lord, but what of the UO? I grow tired of their arrogance."

"As do I", Narel replies, "but we must stay the course my friend. Contact Moab and make sure all outposts are on schedule.

This time we give them no chance, once the dust settles my military won't have any enemies left strong enough to oppose us."

Demos replies, "The UO may have been blind to us before, but they are not stupid. Within the past few years they have uncovered more knowledge about our operation than they had obtained in decades beforehand. We are being increasingly exposed with every second that passes; first our impediment in taking the golden city, then the loss of a vital infidisk by the highest of Sirian Commanders, the UO's sudden ability to obtain substantial information about our identities and operations is disconcerting to say the least. That's not to mention the numerous small defeats we've suffered across the Verse as of late. On top of all this, we don't have the Org to deflect attention anymore. They were only a few steps behind you today a..."

"They got lucky today you fool", Narel interrupts, "a pair of undercover soldiers happened to be stationed where I was docked…nothing more. As for those other failures, they are insignificant. This plan was created so that once it was placed into effect there would be no chance of disruption. The only thing that can halt its success would be impatience on our part. We have come this far my disciple, do not be ignorant to the present simply because you would like vindication for the past. We have done much over our time together and we will do so much more, just let the plan unfold as we have for so long now. Validation, victory, and revenge are in our future, and in their last moments all who opposed us will beg for forgiveness, to which we will laugh at their pleas. It's just a matter of time my friend. Now leave me, I need rest."

As Brutus and Mace return home and dock their small fleet on Utopera, Brutus is surprised to see that there is no escort waiting to bring him before command. He had thought for sure that Major Veela would have a detainment crew waiting for him. As they complete their landing and exit the ship; Mace, Brutus, and other members of the fleet notice that most of the docking crew is missing and things are unusually quiet for the busy hangar. Brutus thanks all of his soldiers and dismisses them to their quarters, he also has Sergeant Tailkon taken back to his bunk, where he can sleep off the remaining effects of that tranquillizer.

As Brutus and Mace leave the hangar bay and pass through the halls of the UO base, their attention is taken by a large group gathered inside one of the training rooms. There looks to be several hundred maybe even a thousand soldiers packed into the room. The two soldiers are confused so they peer in to get a better look. They can see that the front training room wall has been filled with pictures and letters. A Tringalean private with tears in his eyes emerges from the crowd and walks up to the doors where Mace and Brutus stand. They make way to let him pass and Mace curiously asks, "What happened private?"

The soldier gives a despondent look, "Narel happened. Commander Pollah and most of his fleet were wiped out trying to engage him on Prospina. The sick warmonger launched every nuke he had at close range, that maniac doesn't even care about the lives of his own soldiers." The private takes a second to wipe the tears from his eyes. "We aren't even sure yet of who exactly was part of Pollah's fleet. My wife was assigned to it for the past few months, stationed aboard the Olymus, but she was ordered to be transferred two days ago and they don't have any idea whether or not she was there."

He begins to cry even more, "I have to go."

"Hang in there", Mace says to him, "keep hope brother".

The soldier then walks away in despair.

"How can this happen?" Brutus says to Mace, "even Narel, how could he sacrifice so many of his own?"

Mace replies, "It's no sacrifice if you don't value the offering. Narel is unlike any other enemy we've ever faced. He's one step ahead at all times and he has no emotion, no conscience, and essentially no weaknesses. He'll make the selfish decision in order for self preservation every time, no matter who or how many casualties result."

"I'm going to see Major Parra", Brutus says. "Maybe he can let me in on the full story. You should probably head to the medical
bay."

"I hope you're joking?" Mace replies, "do you really think I can heal with something like this hanging over my head? Let's find out what happened."

The two soldiers make their way over to Major Parra's quarters where they receive word that he is attending a ceremony just down the hall in one of the officer's assembly rooms. He and his wife are mourning the loss of her father, leader of the fallen fleet, Commander Pollah. The two rush over to the assembly hall, oblivious to the fact that a full blown memorial for the Commander and the lost fleet is already taking place. As they realize at the last moment what they're walking in on, Mace and Brutus stop at the door. There are a couple hundred family members and friends packed within the large, auditorium-like room including several commanders as well as dozens of officers accompanied by their families. Some are standing or kneeling, but most sit, attentively listening to Major Parra who's volunteered to speak on the tragedy. He sees Mace and Brutus enter and motions them to sit down. They do so as the Major continues...

"The courageous people we lost today were unaware of the fate that awaited them. They were simply reporting for a normal assignment like any other day in the past; nothing could have prepared them for what was to come. The truth we must realize however is that we are at war now, as we have been with Narel for what seems like all of time. A constant threat who uses deception as his primary tactic, his extinction can never be trusted. This persistent nemesis is both unpredictable and uncontrollable. He is a plague to this Universe that always seems to re-emerge, and if not stopped, I fear these won't be the only soldiers we're holding memorials for.

Even so, Narel isn't nearly as smart as he thinks. For the past few centuries he's remained hidden; his existence concealed in folklore and rumors, always deemed untrue by those in authority. Now, we all know the true reality, we all know who did this. You see he made a grave mistake today my friends, because now we won't only be fighting for ourselves, we won't be fighting for the people of the Verse, we won't even be fighting simply because it's right...now above all other reasoning, we'll do it for the ones we lost...Because no matter what happens after this, or how much he suffers, we can never bring them back. And that's why we're going to win, because what he fights for doesn't even compare."

The Major leaves the stage to a brief but hefty applause as another officer steps up to address the crowd. He consoles his wife and children for a moment before excusing himself to speak with Mace and Brutus. The two wait patiently until the Major reaches them, "Mace, I have to say it's good to see you back, I guess something positive came from this day after all. I can't wait to hear how you've pulled off this latest miracle but as I'm sure you know
by now this isn't the time."

Mace replies, "We heard Major and I'm sorry to interrupt, but what exactly happened?"

The Major highlights the encounter, "You knew Privates Gaaron and Uren, correct?"

"Of course", says Brutus, "since the Sirian War."

"They were fine soldiers", replies the Major, "stationed on Prospina to watch the spaceports and cities for suspected Nexcin activity. Low and behold, true to his usual unpredictability, Narel shows up himself and docks his ship at exactly the spaceport where our soldiers are posted. They make him, confirm ID with us, and the rest is history. You know how Narel operates; he had no chance against Pollah's fleet, so he nuked his way out."

Brutus replies, "I can't believe with the manhunt we have going he can simply pop up on Prospina. Decades without a single verified sighting and he still finds ways to travel the Verse; out in the open just like that."

"I don't understand", says Mace, "if they ID'd him and reported it why didn't our units just land in force and pin him in. There's no reason for an individual team to confront him."

"That was the original plan", the Major replies, "but before the fleet was in position to deploy, Narel must've caught wind of what was going on and killed both Gaaron and Uren. Their bodies were found inside the spaceport. He then broke his starship off from the repair bay, breaching two docking blocks and taking thousands of innocent crew members against their will. Once free from the repair port he makes a dash to escape, soon realizing that they're trapped however, he devises his catastrophic assault."

Mace thinks for a moment and replies, "It just doesn't make sense. Narel couldn't have recognized the team, they were both too young to be profiled or identified as UO, and if the warlord had been worried about being discovered on Prospina they never would have landed there to begin with. The UO wasn't in range to be detected by any of his instruments, so unless they caught wind of a transmission how did he know we were coming? How did he know?"

The Major thinks, "Well they maintained air-wave silence, but..." The Major can't think of anything, stumped he says, "Well, Narel is always that one step ahead, you know that better then anyone."

"Yea", Mace replies, "but it can always be explained afterward, his reasoning and actions always accounted for and understood.

Something's different this time though, he was rushed and sloppy. He left the ship for repairs and all intentions show that he had no idea of what was coming. Then mysteriously, out of nowhere he's onto us once again. He goes assassin, emerges seemingly without cause and murders our ground team."

Major Parra inquisitively asks, "What are you getting at?"

"I'm not sure yet", Mace replies, "and trust me you don't wanna

know until I am. But don't worry Major, I feel like after today the odds are a little more in our favor."

The Major responds, "Good, keep that frame of mind because right after word of the tragedy got out an emergency council session was held and I was put in charge of the UO's new focus investigation. Uncover and determine the extent of Narel's following and infrastructure by any means necessary. We have authority over half of the UO's field agents, I'm putting you two in command of major operations."

Mace humbly replies, "Thank you Major. It's sad that it takes something like this to open our eyes sometimes".

"Yea", the Major replies, "well now all eyes are on us, and we're getting the shot we've been asking for. So let's go get him."